MW00364589

THE UNSELECTED JOURNALS

OF

Emma M. Lion

VOL. 3

BETH BROWER

THE UNSELECTED JOURNALS OF *Emma M. Lion*

Rhysdon Press

This is a work of fiction. Names, characters, places and incidents either are the product of the author's imagination or are used fictitiously. Any resemblances to actual persons, living or dead, events, business establishments, or locales is entirely coincidental.

write@bethbrower.com

Published by Rhysdon Press
Printed in the United States of America

Publishers Cataloging-in-Publication data. Brower, Beth.
The Unselected Journals of Emma M. Lion, Vol. 3: Beth Brower; p.cm.
ISBN 978-0-9980636-3-8 1. Fiction Historical 2. Fiction. I. Title.

10 9 8 7 6 5 4 3 2

978-0-9980636-3-8

Text was set in Baskerville

Emma M. Lion
would like to dedicate her journals to all those
who have the presumption to read them.

She understands the temptation to do so.

And while no good may come of such an indiscretion,
one is bound to have a jolly amount of fun.

PREVIOUSLY MENTIONED PERSONS OF INTEREST

Emma M. Lion – *Myself, obviously. Reclaiming Lapis Lazuli House.*

Archibald Flat – *Cheat, thief, villain. General plague on mankind.*

Cousin Matilde – *Archibald's older sister. Dragon of a woman.*

Lady Eugenia Spencer – *Formidable Aunt. Loyal if not Affectionate.*

Damian Spencer – *Older cousin. Currently hiding on the Continent.*

Arabella Spencer – *Goddess Divine. Golden Beauty. Fellow Conspirator.*

Parian – *Valet, Butler, Intolerable Man. Lazy to boot.*

Agnes – *Maid, Cook. Underpaid. Odd opinions. Scottish. Wonderful.*

Niall Pierce – *The Tenant. Proven Pyramus. Mystery still abounds.*

Young Hawkes – *'Mighty Nigel Hawkes'. St. Crispian's unlikely vicar.*

Duke of Islington – *Disapproving. Well educated, I believe.*

The Roman – *St. Crispian's resident ghost, whom I've yet to see in person.*

Mary Bairrage – *Fellow survivor of Fortitude, A Preparatory School for Girls.*

Jack Hollingstell – *Mary's pretend cousin. Scoundrel. Owed two favours.*

Roland Sutherland – *Childhood nemesis turned gorgeous Sun God.*

Saffronia March – *Old Friend. Artist. Painting in Italy.*

Phineas & Oliver Brookstone – *Twins. Fleeing marriage. Jolly good fun.*

Miss Hunt – *Unlikable. Husband hunting. Her sights set on Roland.*

George West – *Possible husband for Arabella. Loves maps and sweet peas.*

Charles Goddard – *Tall, skinny, flagpole. My unintended intended.*

Evelyn Stuart – *Maxwell's older brother.*

Maxwell Stuart – *January 31st 1861 –July 27th 1880*

July 1st

A noise woke me from my dreams this morning. I lay curled beneath my blanket in the dark, eyes closed, in a general—and what would prove temporary—sense of well-being. Upon hearing the noise a second time, I batted my eyes open and scrunched the blanket away from my face. Nightmare of all nightmares, there stood an apparition peering over me in the near dark, a shiny nose beneath a bent set of spectacles. The nose I had seen before, the spectacles I had not.

Proud as I may not be to admit what happened next, I am committed to the truth.

I screamed.

And Cousin Archibald flew backward, flapping in his silk morning robe.

"Cousin Archibald!" I ~~stated calmly~~ shouted. "What are you doing here?"

He spent *several* seconds shushing me, holding his finger to his lips and blowing spittle from his mouth. "Shush! Shush! Quiet down!"

"I will not!" I answered, pulling my blanket to my chin for Decency's Sake. "Why are you in my room!"

His face was bright scarlet, and he looked as if he wanted to bash me on the head. "You'll wake The Tenant!"

"He'll survive," I snapped. "Now, what in heaven's name are you doing?"

My assumption was revenge, for having put an end to his ruinous meddling in my life.

Archibald straightened himself and wiped his mouth with the sleeve of his purple morning robe. "I wanted to let you know I intend to accompany you to church."

"Church?" said I.

"Yes, church," answered he.

"The religious meeting that begins at eleven o'clock?" pressed I.

"Yes," confirmed he.

"The one where morality, honesty, and selflessness are discussed?"

"Yes. The very same."

At which moment I refrained from scoffing. Only just.

"What time is it now, Cousin?"

"Half-past four," stated he.

I collapsed back onto my bed and, as it was the Sabbath, uttered a prayer for the demon to leave me be. Upon reopening one eye, I saw my petition had gone up in vain. Cousin Archibald was still standing in my room.

"Why are you telling me you wish to attend church at half-past four in the morning?"

"We must arrive early," came his reply.

"Why?" I demanded, resisting the urge to strangle the old man.

"It's July the First!" he screamed with near desperation.

"Shh!" I whispered in return. "Yes, I was very much alive for the month of June, despite your best efforts. We can both agree it is July the first. Now, what is your point?"

"You are a *heathen*!" said he, with venom.

Venom, says I.

And then it dawned. Not literally, no. It was still well before dawn, and I've not forgiven Archibald for it. Rather, my mind was illuminated.

"It is July the first." I put my head in my hands. "No wonder you're acting like a lunatic."

"We have to be clever if we are to secure the prize!"

"We?" I looked up at this man who had taken my financial security and smothered it at the racetrack with silk morning robes. Who had done all he could to bring about my failure. Who will most likely be well satisfied to see me end in the gutter. Archibald Flat, this bitter, ridiculous caricature of a human being. "We?" I repeated. "You think—after what you have done to me—that I will help you? It's a miracle I haven't thrown you out!"

In one unexpected sweep of emotion, Archibald embodied both pride and defeat. "I can't do it on my own anymore," he admitted, his voice shaking. "I've tried, and I can't. Your father used to help me, but he is no longer. I miss it every year, my *favourite* thing." And then he lifted a shaking hand to brush his wild hair away from his forehead. I thought it was to reveal The Scar, but the man blinked several times, eyes shimmering like glass.

He was trying not to cry.

The self-righteous indignation in my chest was pricked and then partially deflated. I am not beyond being moved by the pathetic, and Cousin Archibald is nothing if not that.

It was with a sigh that I asked, "Do you think the clue will be given at church?"

"Yes, yes!" His recovery was suspiciously swift. "It always *is*, when the first is a Sunday!"

It was a moment of judgement. Poor judgement.

Throw my fate in with Cousin Archibald? Or refuse on principle? My childhood visits being in June, this year is my first First. But my father loved the game as a younger man. I blame this moment of sentimentality for my agreeing that we venture forth as partners.

"Then we should arrive well before eleven o'clock."

"Yes, yes!"

"Does Agnes know to prepare breakfast early?"

"I've already woken her."

"Poor girl! When on earth do you wish to leave?"

"Six o'clock."

I rubbed my eyes in an effort to refrain from strangling the man. "Cousin, I will be ready to leave for church at half past nine and not a minute before."

"But—!"

"If you wish to go earlier and save a place, you are more than welcome to do so. I will arrive an hour and a half before the service, extreme by almost any measure. Now, away with you. Out of my room."

Bunching his face into the semblance of a sad prune, Cousin Archibald fought only a moment before accepting his fate. "The young generation is a *weak* generation, and it will all go to the dogs when your kind take power."

"My kind?"

But he had stomped out.

I lay in bed divided between the very human emotions of annoyance, curiosity, and betrayal against myself for helping that man with anything.

When I finally did leave my bed, two sleepless hours later, I washed, dressed, and pinned my hair as best I could—Agnes deserving not to be bothered again.

The Tenant was awake, and so I sent him a missive.

> *My apologies if you were disturbed in the ungodly hours of the morning.*

Agnes brought me breakfast on a tray—fruit, toast, ham—and as I ate, a note was passed back through the wall.

> *I WAS AWAKE.*

Does the man ever sleep?

I did not ask, as I do have *some* sense of propriety—a loose definition, granted.

As I ate my toast and gazed at my Shakespeare-laden bookshelf, I could hear Mr. Pierce moving through his morning ablutions. Then the door of his closet opened, and Tybalt slipped past the small curtain that hangs over his personal door in the wall, crossing the room without so much as a greeting and commandeering my unmade bed.

He is a very spoilt creature.

"Good morning, Tybalt."

Tybalt's ear moved in my direction at the mention of his name, but he was already halfway into a curl and settled down with no other recognition of my person, his tail twitching.

It was then that Mr. Pierce put on his boots.

I know this because while the sound that travels between our shared wall is muffled—except, I imagine, for screaming lunatics in the wee hours of the morning—it is easier to hear his footsteps when he's wearing boots. They serve as a map of his movements.

I cannot say why I like the phenomena, but I do. Heavy footfalls, abrupt stops, all punctuating his mysterious life on the other side of the wall.

I digress.

Mr. Pierce walked over to his desk—boots!—and a moment later, another note was slipped through the wall.

> *ARE YOU WELL THIS MORNING, MISS LION?*

> *I am, thank you.*

Considering he'd never begun a conversation of any sort—in person or via wall communications—by asking "Are you well?" I added,

> *Why do you ask?*

> *I HEARD YOU CRY OUT AND WAS READY TO TAKE ACTION UNTIL I HEARD MR. FLAT SCREAM. AT WHICH POINT I FIGURED YOU HAD THE SITUATION IN HAND.*
>
> *ALSO, YOU DID NOT ASK WHY I WAS AWAKE AT SAID UNGODLY HOUR. NOR DID YOU EXPLAIN THE CAUSE OF COMMOTION. IN OUR BRIEF, YET STORIED, ACQUAINTANCE, I WOULD HAZARD YOU TO ALREADY HAVE DONE BOTH.*
>
> *ERGO, ARE YOU WELL THIS MORNING?*

> *What a summation of my character! As for the incident in question, I had it quite in hand. As for asking after your personal sleeping habits, that could be construed as impertinent. And as impertinence comes in limited supply (one has only so much in any given day), it's unwise to spend it all before breakfast.*

I HAVE NO QUALMS USING MINE EARLY. WHY THE COMMOTION?

It's July the first, in St. Crispian's.

MEANING?

Meaning that in fifteen days there will be a production of Julius Caesar *somewhere in the neighbourhood. No one, excepting the committee—a shadow affair whose members remain a secret—knows who will play what parts or where it will take place. There are limited tickets, and one must follow the clues to secure them before they are gone. It is one of the grand traditions of our St. Crispian's year.*

As it is a Sunday, the first clue will be hidden in the sermon. Mr. Flat wants to make certain we arrive at church early.

AMATEURS FROM ST. CRISPIAN'S HAVE ONLY FIFTEEN DAYS TO PREPARE A PERFORMANCE OF JULIUS CAESAR, *AND YOU ARE WAKING UP BEFORE DAWN IN HOPES OF WATCHING SUCH A DISASTER?*

My cry of indignation was likely heard through the wall. It was then my passion for the project grew out of hand.

Mr. Pierce, have some reverence! Having performed this play for well over one hundred years, I assure you, we are up for the task. Amateurs? Not so! Our humble neighbourhood has killed Caesar more effectively than anyone else in the world.

Repeatedly.

To quote The Bard, "How many ages hence shall this our lofty scene be acted over, in states unborn and accents yet unknown!"

Also, this is my first July in St. Crispian's. It is a banner moment in my life.

Amateurs indeed.

I ASK YOUR PARDON AND WISH YOU LUCK.

Thank you.

Also be warned: Our fellow St. Crispians may spontaneously quote Julius Caesar *at you.*

I AM WARNED.

Later

Young Hawkes, for all his going about and doing good, has a rather devious sense of humour. The church was full to bursting when he stood to deliver his sermon. Archibald sat beside me, perched on the edge of the pew like a hatchling about to fling itself out of the nest. I sighed, tried not to be embarrassed by my company, and focused on Hawkes, who stood for a full minute without speaking, a gleam of something untoward in his eye. Then he began the longest sermon he has ever given. We were herrings in a barrel with no hope of escape. It went on not for an hour, or even two, but *three*. He spoke—in detail—about each of the Ten Commandments and then spent a good deal of time in the New Testament. It appeared he was amusing himself greatly at our expense. The weak-stomached left shortly after midday. The weak-hearted not long after. But a great many of us stuck it through to the bitter end, and bitter it was, for there was nothing in the entire sermon that could be considered the first clue. Finally, as it was nearing two o'clock, he said in an uncommitted voice: "I am a surgeon to old souls: when they are in great danger, I recover them."

I elbowed Cousin Archibald in the ribs.

"What?! What?!" he said.

"Shhh!" I lifted a finger to my mouth. "He just said, 'I am a surgeon to old souls.'"

"The cobbler? The cobbler says that in act one."

"Precisely."

Archibald straightened in a superior manner. "The cobbler in the play says 'shoes' not 'souls.' I've the entire play memorized. That cannot be our clue."

It was a moment of unbearable stupidity.

"It's not meant to be an exact quote, Cousin. Young Hawkes was tailoring it to himself. It's a play on words. *Sole* of the shoe. *Soul* of mankind. Do you see?"

He furrowed his brow and nodded. Then, without waiting for Young Hawkes to finish his sermon, Archibald stood, impolitely forced himself past the others sitting on our pew, and left the church.

I could have sworn Hawkes raised an eyebrow in my direction.

July 2nd

According to what I recall my father saying, the key to securing a ticket to *Julius Caesar* is to not let it be known that one is trying to secure a ticket to *Julius Caesar*. One is to appear nonchalant while giving every ounce of attention to following each clue.

It is the Art of Appearing Disinterested.

Yesterday, after grudgingly accepting the terms for us working together—namely, that there shall be no attempt to kill or maim one Emma M. Lion, also that he is to hold his tongue—Cousin Archibald and I decided we should begin at the Philosopher's Sole, Cordwainer and Cobbler, seeing as how Young Hawkes had quoted the cobbler from the play.

Cousin Archibald was determined to wait outside on the walk until it opened. Although he did not believe me, I attempted to explain that it would be seen as gauche by the other clue seekers.

"Subtlety is the tradition, Cousin, and I will not arrive at Philosopher's Sole before it opens. We will take a pair of shoes to be repaired at nine o'clock sharp. As if we had meant to stop by all along."

I cannot claim to have rested well last night. Archibald has been acting like a child only days away from summer holiday, a thing which is catching even if said child is rotten and unprincipled.

It is now quarter to nine in the morning, and I am waiting in the drawing room—my old boots ready for repair. Archibald is to meet me. I am hoping ~~we both make it through~~ I make it through this partnership alive.

Ah, there it is. The sound of doom descending the staircase.

Later

Archibald Flat was not created for stealth of any kind.

The events of the morning have proven it thus.

He came into the drawing room this morning, rocking back and forth on his feet while I gathered my things, running his fingers against the silk morning robe he had beneath his coat. One might ask the very valid question of how he has managed to fit an entire silk morning robe in his trousers? Well. It seems he cut the bottom half of the morning robe clean off, so as to provide "the comfort of one's bedroom in the street." Or so he told me. He calls it his Out and About Reminder.

It is somewhat alarming to find this likeable oddity in my cousin. Anyone who calls anything their "Out and About Reminder" must have a sliver of poetry in their soul. A *sliver*. The smallest measure. The rest of Archibald's soul is dismal soot grey, I am convinced.

As I was closing my journal, Archibald said, "What is *that*?"

"My personal journal," I replied, tucking it away quickly.

Archibald then cleared his throat and said, "Matilde told me you engaged in the filthy habit."

Filthy habit?

The accusation makes me eager to reread my journal in case I've missed something marvellous.

There was a knot of customers at Philosopher's, looking as casually about their business as possible, shoes in hand. Mr. Argyll played he was upset with the crowd—adjusting his glasses, alternately ordering and disordering his greying hair with a repeated pass of his hand—but one can only guess this is good for business. When it was finally our turn to be served, I placed my pair of boots on the counter, and Archibald made the addition of gently used shoes in no need of repair.

Mr. Argyll nodded. "How may I help you?"

"Quickly man, give us the clue," Archibald said, a bit too loudly.

"I've no idea what you mean," Mr. Argyll answered with disapproval

"Come along," Archibald continued. "Here are boots and shoes. Don't keep me dawdling. It's a highway robbery as it is."

That was when I elbowed my elderly cousin and hissed that perhaps he would like to wait outside.

Once Archibald had stomped away, I turned my sweetest smile on Mr. Argyll. "A pair of boots, in need of repair. And shoes, in lesser need."

Nodding, Mr. Argyll wrote down the information for our order and then asked, "Are you above reproach, young miss?"

Clearly a clue. Only I was uncertain of how to answer.

I settled on ineloquent, sporting with dim-witted.

"I, um, yes?"

He blinked at me.

I thought through the lines of the play in question and answered in the words of Caesar's wife, "I am above reproach to some, Mr. Argyll. I'm afraid others would dispute the fact."

His nod was almost imperceptible. "Pick up your boots tomorrow, and I will have something for you."

We went home. Cousin Archibald, having worked his temper into what one might call a frenzy, yelled for quarter of an hour how my incompetence was going to cost us the first clue, that it was criminal we should wait until tomorrow, and that I was worthless.

My answer was to remind him that, as per our agreement, he was to hold his tongue.

Up the stairs he marched.

I stood there thinking that if I were wise, I would dissolve the absurd partnership immediately.

Once the man retreated to the locked doors of the second floor, I said to Agnes, who was standing in the hall wringing her hands, "You do see, Agnes, the Ill Logic that is Mr. Archibald Flat?"

Agnes frowned. "My mother might say he was troubled and in need of divine intervention, Miss Lion. But I don't like to speak ill of the living."

My smile came with a raised eyebrow. "That is usually reserved for the dead. What of them?"

"Oh, I don't think they mind a few snippy words now and again."

Perhaps not, Agnes.

July 3rd

I just woke to find a note slipped beneath my door. It is written in a craggy, self-absorbed hand and informs me that I am to *wait.* Under no circumstance am I to do anything which could jeopardize the campaign. I am to remain at home as, and I quote, "a proper woman should," while Cousin Archibald retrieves his shoes from Philosopher's and returns with the clue.

Well.

Shoddy timing for striking out on his own, as we are racing the entire neighbourhood.

Wishing the fool good luck, I am going to address my correspondence, which includes—I admit it is a thing which causes delight—a question slipped through the wall a few moments ago.

> *I'VE A MIND TO BEGIN WORK ON THE STUDIO TODAY. SEEING AS HOW THERE IS NO DOOR YET BETWEEN THE SALON AND LAPIS LAZULI MINOR, I WAS HOPING TO ENTER THROUGH LAPIS LAZULI HOUSE. UNLESS, OF COURSE, YOU WISH ME TO TAKE A SLEDGEHAMMER TO THE WALL, SIGHT UNSEEN.*

> *However tempting the prospect of sitting on the sofa and watching you battle your way through, I will let you in via Lapis Lazuli House. My morning is suddenly come free because I am ordered to be A Proper Woman for at least a few hours. I humour he who gave me such an order, not because he holds any authority, but because I expect him to fail spectacularly at what he has set out to do alone and the less genteel part of my nature wants for amusement.*

He took it back! Mr. Pierce slipped a response through the wall just now, and as I reached for it, he took it back!

Not having established Rules of Order for Garret Communication in The Year of 1883, I don't know the legality of such an action.

I told him so.

Can one withdraw a communication? It feels as if you've cheated something.

CERTAINLY. THE POWER TO WITHDRAW MUST BE AN UNSPOKEN RIGHT.

IF YOU WERE TOO SLOW TO CLAIM THE COMMUNICATION, AND IT WAS WITHIN MY POWER TO REMOVE, THERE SHOULD BE NO PROHIBITION ON THE ACT.

Unspoken Right? Power to Remove? You're sounding rather American.

THEY HAVE THEIR USES.

Americans?

RIGHTS

I MUST CONCEDE, THERE ARE SOME VERY FINE AMERICANS.

How very un-British of you.

WE CAN'T ALL BE AS PROPER AS MISS LION.

Later

The day has been too long and yet pleasant.

The "too long" due to Cousin Archibald.

The "pleasant" to Mr. Pierce.

After our debate concerning Rules of Order for Garret Communication in The Year of 1883—Mr. Pierce still has not told me what the original missive said—I went downstairs.

Agnes, when she heard whom I was expecting, had paled and fled to the kitchen. Parian was busy—actually busy—in the back garden, where I had tasked him to wrestle Eden into submission if he valued his life, his post, or his comfortable third floor rooms.

Thus, it was left to myself to open the door when the knock came. I did, and there was Mr. Pierce. A summer storm, as he stood on my stoop in his unintended but brooding manner. I could almost smell the rain.

"Come in, Mr. Pierce."

"Thank you."

When he entered the hall, it brought that May dinner to mind.

I cringed. But then the thought of Cousin Archibald standing on his chair charmed a smile.

Mr. Pierce made comment.

"Are you amused by something?" he said.

I could have lied and said, "A pleasant morning, is all."

Alas, honesty won the day. "I was thinking of our disastrous dinner. Very gallant of you to have forgiven me."

"It was…memorable. Have you had any more visits from your ghost?"

"The Roman? I believe he's been spending his time on Traitors Road."

"Pity." But it did not sound like Mr. Pierce meant it.

I turned the knob, pushed the door open, and we entered the salon. All but one of the curtains were closed, yet the dust was still evident.

"Oh dear. I should have Agnes come clean the room for you."

He walked past me. "No need, Miss Lion. If I'm to install a new door and paint the room, I anticipate a bit of a mess. Once I'm finished, perhaps I'll pay Agnes to help clean, if she has the inclination and the time. With your permission, of course."

Agnes would rather die, I thought.

"Certainly, I'll ask her," I said. "You will paint, then?"

To which he answered, "Yes, if you don't mind."

"Not at all," I told him. "I look forward to the change. I like yellow, as a rule, but it doesn't seem to complement this room very well. It is a bit ghastly, like a wizened old man insisting everyone be happy. "

"It is a touch Italian for me. Lovely in Venice, not my cup of tea in London."

Venice.

He said the word with such an offhand tone. As if it was so common a reference.

I am—understandably so, I defend—very curious about these patchwork pieces of his past.

"And what of New York?"

He was walking about the salon at that point, and answered, "What of New York?"

"Did you keep a studio?"

"Of sorts."

"What was the colour?"

"Deep red."

How he said the words made his former studio sound like another woman. Meaning, a woman in general. Not *another* woman. Heavens. He would have to have one in the first place to have another, wouldn't he?

Keeping such thoughts to myself, I asked, "Will you paint this studio red, then?"

"No, I've something else in mind: what I would have done in New York had I these windows."

"Oh?" It was an invitation for him to tell me his intended colour. Instead, he walked towards the wall that separated the salon from Lapis Lazuli Minor, his storm cloud eyes catching the light from the windows.

"Our shared wall in the garret is clearly lacking in quality, but this looks solid. Seeing as it is not weight-bearing, I should be able to put in a door easily enough." He knocked about on the wall. "I think about here? If it suits, Miss Lion. The trick will be to find a door that will sufficiently match the one that leads into your hall."

And there it was, my moment of brilliance. For I recalled having had to shift a door in my sorting of the west garret.

"Allow me to come to your aid," I said. "I have a door that matches all the others in the house. It's up in the garret. You're most welcome to use it, but I will need your help bringing it down as it is quite heavy. Solid wood, only the best, and all that. I figure you should be able to manage it, seeing as how you are very…" I paused then. It was an angular place to stop. A great deal more awkward than I intended, followed by the terrible fear I was turning into Agnes. Seeing as how I was not going to say what I was really thinking, I finished with the word "…tall."

Very tall.

Seeing as how you are very tall.

What a triumph you are, Emma M. Lion.

Mr. Pierce had given me his attention as soon as I'd started speaking, and with each additional sentence the side of his mouth seemed to rise, his eyes narrowing in proportion, until it was either disbelief or amusement written on his face when I finally arrived at the word Tall.

"Right, then," he answered. "Should we sort it now?"

"Certainly."

I stood there a moment while I tried to remember if the west garret was too much of a mess with my personal things. Alas, it was too late to withdraw the invitation. I might have said it was not an ideal time and that I would have Parian help bring the door down; then I thought of Parian—thin frame of a shallow man that he is, handling four sets of stairs—and decided Mr. Pierce was for the best.

Stockings thrown over rubbish be damned.

Hmm. The above language is shocking.

Should it be struck from the record?

I say no. If it is in the Bible, it can certainly be written in my journal.

Not that I intend to stake any man's head to the ground…which would be very Old Testament.

I digress.

We left the salon. I led the way up the four flights of stairs. Mr. Pierce was not directly beside me, nor directly behind me, rather at a diagonal, as if we were co-conspiring pieces on a chessboard. A strange sort of camaraderie.

Between the third and fourth floor it struck me that when one's neighbour has a mysterious and clearly painful limp, one ought to have enquired if managing a heavy door would suit.

Unless that would wound his pride.

Even at the risk of greater injury to his leg.

There seemed no way of bringing the matter forward without calling into question his capabilities.

Which might result in him calling me out.

I would accept, and ask Agnes to be my second.

Mr. Pierce and I would duel in the street.

I would die.

Someone would write a verse commemorating the event.

Mr. Pierce, somewhat regretful, would carry—limping all the while—the door down and drape it with a black ribbon, wishing his pride had not consumed his actions.

Alas.

We must all live with our choices…

By the time we had passed the fourth floor, I decided to allow the man to make his own judgement concerning his fitness for the task.

Thus I retained my young life.

Having ascended the mount, we came to the landing to find the door of the west garret closed, while the door to the east garret was halfway ajar. There was no way to gracefully close it; and seeing as how there was nothing incriminating in sight—only one edge of the rug, with the chair and its mismatched cushions, and the full window beyond—I motioned towards it and said, "The inner sanctum."

"Colourful cushions. I didn't imagine the walls painted white." Then, "Where's the door?"

Well. If that's as far as his curiosity extends…

Opening the door to the west garret, I motioned for him to precede me through the doorway.

He did, then stopped so abruptly I almost ran into him.

"I am sorely tempted to fetch my camera," Mr. Pierce said, mostly to himself.

I glanced around him, trying to see what had caught his vision.

An attic of hideaway places and old stories, odd shapes, with only one and a half windows to give shape and form. Mr. Pierce stepped further into the garret, and I leaned against the door frame, watching his enjoyment.

I had forgotten what it is like to live with an artist. The unexpected pauses over what might be considered mundane to most.

It is a bittersweet reminder.

My father would do that to my mother and myself all the time. Something would strike him, and he couldn't let it be until he had captured it in a sketchbook. Then, months later, I would catch glimpses of it in the newspaper or next to a story in a magazine.

I enjoyed the unexpected rush of memory, when life was happy in an uncomplicated way, and managed to smile over it, but beneath the smile, I felt wistful.

After a few moments, motion returned to the room—Mr. Pierce stepping through the clutter, tactfully ignoring the open wardrobe with my day dresses and gowns looking as undisciplined as their owner. I pointed towards the corner behind a desk, two crates, and some picture frames, where the door lay on its side.

Between the two of us, we made quick work clearing a path, and when I was about to propose we each take an end and go slowly, he bent down, raised the door enough to slip his left hand beneath and, standing, lifted it with far more ease than I had been capable.

"Lead on, Miss Lion."

So I did.

Back down the stairs we went (Mr. Pierce taking extra care not to bash the walls, bless him), and when we entered the salon, he set it against the wall with a masculine sound and stood up, brushing his hands.

"Well done," I said.

"Before I forget—" And he withdrew an envelope from his pocket. "Rent for the studio, for six months. As well as Lapis Lazuli Minor. That should see me through the end of the year on both counts."

The envelope felt rather full.

It was then that Parian knocked on the door. Fresh out of the garden, his hands were still covered in dirt, as if he were an explorer just come from the bush. "I was sent to fetch you to the drawing room," he huffed.

"Thank you, Parian. You've had a lovely start to taming the garden."

His answer was nonverbal, and possibly insulting.

"If there's anything else you need, Mr. Pierce," I said.

"I'll let myself out in a few minutes, Miss Lion. Then, if you don't mind, I'll begin on the doorway later today or tomorrow."

"Of course."

Entering the drawing room, my hand strategically holding the envelope behind my back, I found Archibald sitting at the round table by the window.

"He wouldn't give me the clue," said he.

"Pardon?"

I sat down in the chair opposite.

Archibald ran a greasy hand over his face and made a strange growling sound. "Mr. Argyll. I demanded, but he is an imbecile. Didn't understand a thing I was shouting."

I weighed with careful consideration whether I should explain how human relations manage to limp along, not shouting being a key component. Deciding it would be a waste of time, I stood and said, "I will go now."

"Yes, let us," answered he, reaching for his hat.

"No, Cousin Archibald. I will go. You will remain. As a proper man should," insisted I, with a smile.

It was not returned.

Going upstairs and hiding Mr. Pierce's rent money under my mattress—how desperately orphan of me—I changed from my old frock to my bottle-green day dress. Finding my hat and pair of gloves, I set out. Arriving at Philosopher's, I enquired if my cousin had already picked up my boots with his shoes.

"Only his own," Mr. Argyll answered. "Said you would pay for both pairs."

"Did he?"

"I wouldn't have it. Made him pay for his shoes."

And Mr. Argyll looked at me in a meaningful way and winked, as if we were both spies for the same country and he was trying to give me a signal.

I winked in return.

After I paid for my boots, which now look a good deal more put together than they did when I arrived in London, Mr. Argyll nodded towards the back room and said, "Perhaps you'd like to go and see the Missus? She'd be very happy to speak with you."

I know Mr. Argyll has no wife—unless he is following in the tradition of our beloved Mr. Rochester, keeping her cloistered in the attic.

I have let Jane Eyre go to my head.

I said, "I would be happy to visit."

When I went into the back room, I saw a dressmaker's mannequin costumed like a patrician woman, and at her side a golden bowl filled with marbles and nothing else.

I picked one, a clear green glass, and slipped it into my reticule.

Upon returning home, I found Cousin Archibald fretting in the hall.

"Well!" shouted he.

I withdrew the marble and set it on the side table. Then I had to catch it before it rolled off. "A green marble," said I.

"A marble! Well then, let us be off!"

"Off?"

"About St. Crispian's! We can discuss the marble and look for clues at the same time."

He had, I must concede, a point.

And so off we went.

The two of us stalked all about St. Crispian's—the length of Whereabouts Lane twice, cutting across the Diagonal, up Sterling, around Baron's Square, down Sterling, up Sterling again, along Traitors, into the side streets and back to Whereabouts, where we collapsed at Jacob's Well.

It was quite warm.

He only insulted me on thirteen occasions. I reminded him seven times that he was financially dependent on my generosity, and how, as a blackguard, he should—by all that was good and holy—be cast into the gutter.

He told me not to be vulgar.

I told him he must choose between my vulgarity or my being wilfully cruel, which may or not include sending him to Bournemouth and Cousin Matilde.

He made no answer but brushed his hair aside, so The Scar was on full display.

In the end, all that work for nothing.

Not a sign in a shop window, not a clue set about a house, indicating the meaning of the green marble. Which is now beside me on the desk, looking smug.

I almost called off our ~~foolish~~ ~~precarious~~ perversely trying partnership, but I will own to finding some amusement in the endeavour. In the words of our beloved play, "*Mischief, thou art afoot. Take thou what course thou wilt.*"

We begin again tomorrow.

July 4th

Archibald is spending the day having Parian sing "God Save the Queen" while he—Archibald, not Parian—curses the Colonies. He is also dressed in full mourning.

It is nearly beyond human endurance.

"It's not that I've got anything against the Queen, Miss Lion," Agnes said as she punched bread dough down. "But if I have to hear Parian sing that song one more time..."

I asked Archibald if his inspiration for full mourning was my recent return to London, to which he croaked, "You have nothing to do with it! I have worn full mourning on this day for fifty years!"

"How convenient. If anyone in St. Crispian's were to die, one of us would already be dressed appropriately."

"Have you figured the clue of the green marble?" sneered he as he straightened his black silk morning robe. (Morning robe or *mourning* robe? How is one to know?)

"No, Cousin," answered I. "Have you?" To which his reply was stomping up to the second floor and slamming his bedroom door hard enough to send an echo through the house.

I am now enjoying a cup of tea by myself while staring out the window, feeling remarkably unperturbed. My mad cousin has locked himself in his room. I've a full week of puzzles ahead to earn tickets to *Julius Caesar*. Add a new book, and I would be quite content. Until then, I'm reading the treacherous aforementioned play again.

Strangely enough, *Julius Caesar* is included in *Shakespeare's Comedies, In Full.* The editor who made such a selection sounds like a very dark man, indeed.

Later

Returned from a walk about Primrose Hill just now. As I was crossing the hall, there was significant clatter coming from the salon. Hesitating a moment, I knocked on the door.

The Tenant called, "Come in."

And so I did.

Mr. Pierce had opened the curtains, and the light pouring into the room showed the dust motes floating through the air. A portion of the wall between the salon and Lapis Lazuli Minor had been removed. Mr. Pierce's friend—the one who looks like a pirate—was standing in the dust of it all, his eyepatch slightly askew.

My pleasant smile was met with a scowl.

I suppose when one has a peg leg and an eyepatch, one might scowl. Justifiably so. However, his auburn hair made it difficult to take such an expression with any degree of seriousness.

Be a pirate, if you must, but do not try to do so as a ginger.

I turned my attention to Mr. Pierce, who was standing with a paintbrush in one hand, a small paint can in the other, focused on the wall before him like a soothsayer determined to change the weather.

"What do you think?" he asked without ceremony. There were two colours, patches of charcoal grey and midnight blue.

"Beautiful. Both of them. The blue is especially lovely."

The Pirate grunted, and Mr. Pierce glanced towards him. "Miss Lion, allow me to introduce my friend, Ben Chambers. Chambers, meet Emma Lion."

"Hello," I said.

The Pirate said…nothing. He simply glowered in my general direction. After a prodding look from Mr. Pierce, Mr. Chambers said in a very flat tone, "Pleasure."

Hardly convincing.

I took it upon myself to be graceful. "I see the doorway is"—what I assumed was the doorframe chose that moment to topple to the ground—"coming along."

"I know what I'm doing," growled The Pirate.

"I'm sure you do, Mr. Chambers."

Mr. Pierce smiled as he stepped forward and brushed more paint onto the wall.

And then I said, "I have been meaning to ask you if you wish me to keep this door locked, Mr. Pierce, so that no one from my household can walk into your studio at their leisure?"

He shrugged, stirring the brush into the paint can he held. "No need. If Agnes is to clean it, it would be easy enough to keep the door unlocked. Have you asked her? Besides," he looked towards me, and a drip of paint fell from the brush in his hand without his notice, "how would you visit my studio if I kept it locked?"

"Through your front door, I would presume," I answered. "But I do enjoy the thought of popping in to see what you're about."

A dismissive sound came from The Pirate, at which point I openly stared at him. The man is possibly the rudest I've ever met. Well, saving Archibald.

"How goes your quest?" Mr. Pierce asked. I believe he was redirecting the conversation.

"If you are referring to *Julius Caesar*, the first clue led us to the Philosopher's Sole, where we had to have something repaired. The man, I am certain, has made a small fortune."

"Good for him," Pierce said.

The Pirate rolled his eye and muttered something about degenerate American influences.

Mr. Pierce, ignoring The Pirate, turned his attention back to the paint on the wall. "I can't quite decide between the two."

"Do you shoot the portraits against such dark backgrounds?" I asked.

"Not as often as I'd like. Sometimes," Pierce answered. "I have painted backdrops for the faint of heart. I enjoy a moody portrait, however. A dark wall colour is my preference for most rooms."

Dark, brooding. A touch of the Mr. Rochester.

A thought I had no intention of ever speaking aloud.

Oh, how frail the human tongue…

Sitting down on the plum sofa, set askew in the middle of the room, I crossed my arms and considered each colour.

My suggestion was to flip a coin.

Mr. Pierce looked back at me over his shoulder long enough to say, "I never gamble my decisions, however small."

"Whyever not?" I answered. "Either way the coin falls, you will be pleased with the colour. Still dark. Still brooding. Still Mr. Rochester."

Yes. I said it aloud.

Without thinking.

Appalling.

Mr. Pierce paused, his shoulders tensing. When he turned—slowly—his eyes were narrowed, and there was a dismissive tilt on the side of his mouth. In my defence, there was also a glint in his eyes that can only be attributed to some internal merriment.

"Brooding?" He said. "Rochester? What sort of monster do you paint me to be?"

Monster? No. Certainly not. Mysterious person with a past? Very much yes. It cannot be denied.

"No monster, Mr. Pierce," I said with a nonchalant flip of my hand. It was a bold attempt to cover my own mortification. "For my purposes today, Rochester is only an adjective. He is a mood, a style. Any man who would choose between midnight blue and gunmetal grey opens himself up to such a statement."

The Pirate, whom I should probably refer to by his real name of Chambers, snorted and hit something loudly with his hammer. Mr. Pierce kept his gaze on me. "And if I were to go with another colour altogether, such as a green?"

I thought the answer was fairly obvious.

"Why then we've left Charlotte Brontë entirely and find ourselves in solid Austen territory."

His laugh was swift. "I've never read either, but I think Austen wrote of better men than myself."

"That depends if you are the hero, the villain, or the fool," I replied.

"He's the fool," muttered Chambers from across the room.

Mr. Pierce's mouth pulled tight, and with a side-eye towards his friend, he turned and painted another stripe of blue on the wall.

Well!

Later

Did you decide which paint colour?

NO

AS THE DRAPES ARE RED AND THE SOFA IS PURPLE, AND SEEING AS HOW I HAVE NO INTENTION OF REPLACING THEM, I AM WONDERING WHICH SCHEME WOULD SUIT THE BEST.

Plum

PARDON?

The sofa is plum, not purple.

IS THERE A MEANINGFUL DIFFERENCE?

My father would have said so, yes.

WAS HE IN THE UPHOLSTERY BUSINESS?

No. He was an artist. Now, to your point, I think you should choose the blue. It will balance the warmth of the drapes and upholstery.

THEN I WILL USE THE GREY IN MY WEST GARRET.

Painting two rooms? Your ambition astounds and impresses.

SURVIVAL IS MY MOTIVE.

July 5th

I do not understand the clue of the marble any more than I did yesterday. Feeling the need for conference, I attempted to seek out Archibald. He would not answer his bedroom door.

Alas.

When one dances with a fiend, one finds toes are stepped on.

Having no mandate from Aunt Eugenia, I intend to spend my free morning doing things of import, i.e., attempting to pick the lock on the library door, writing a letter to Saffronia March, and walking about Primrose Hill while carrying the marble in my pocket in hopes lightning will strike.

Later

Speak of the devil and she sendeth a mandate. I returned home to find not one, but two peach envelopes waiting on the table in the hall.

> *Emma,*
>
> *My guests have returned home, and your humble presence is once again necessary. You are, after all, the Foil, however deficient. There are events where you will be required: A dinner at my house, a soirée at the Storidge's, cards at Lord and Lady Black's. But first I expect to see you tomorrow afternoon for tea. Think of your worst qualities and be prepared to discuss what we might do with them.*
>
> *Your Aunt*

My worst qualities? She is ambitious to think we will get through them during only *one* afternoon tea. I should think I require three teas, at least.

Opening the second envelope, I read,

On second thought, I do not wish you to attend Lord and Lady Black's. They have very high standards. I expect you tomorrow at three o'clock sharp.

A small parcel also arrived in today's post, no personal insults attached. It was from Mary and all the Janes of Fortitude, and was wrapped in a lovely striped paper.

Emma,

You have outdone yourself in service to the Jane Eyres of Fortitude. It was decided we would all go in on something fine, in token of your bravery. I hope you enjoy your spoils of war.

Mary

Unwrapping the first gift, I found a gold pen, slim, inscribed with *EML.* Just the right size to carry about.

The second gift, to my delight, is a soft pair of leather gloves. They are the most unusual pale red and will be striking with my day dresses.

They came with a note.

Emma Darling,

I accompanied Mary on her task and selected these red gloves myself. They are to keep you from developing the habit of thievery.

Jack

Scoundrel.

The third and final gift—the proverbial cherry on top—is a beautiful copy of *Jane Eyre*, a single volume edition, soft grey leather with silver ornamentation. It is signed by each of the Janes, in order of their reign. Beautiful and thoughtful.

It looks charmed to be on my shelf.

And I am charmed to have it.

July 6th

Archibald sent Agnes to fetch me before breakfast.

"He said that you've been insolent, Miss Lion, and you are to meet him in the drawing room to discuss the clue."

Insolent?

I exchanged a long-suffering glance with Tybalt, who was curled up on my bed.

"Insolent or indolent, Agnes?" I answered, still dressing for the day. "Are you certain he didn't say indolent?"

Agnes looked at me blankly, then gave her head a shake as she lifted both her shoulders. "I couldn't rightly say, Miss. He said a lot of other words, but I dinnae think my mother would approve of me passing them on, if ya catch my meaning."

I smiled. I love when her Scottish accent isn't too harshly pruned.

Requesting she bring my breakfast to the drawing room, I finished pinning up my hair—in an unflattering way, Aunt Eugenia would say—and descended to Cousin Archibald's level, in every sense of the phrase.

He was sitting at the small round table near one of the front windows looking nervous, his knees bouncing.

"Two days we've had the marble," he sputtered. "Two days. Time is passing! We will spend the entire day walking St. Crispian's until we can figure out what the clue means!"

The spectre of Aunt Eugenia frowning appeared in the corner, and I was forced to admit, "I have a previous engagement, Cousin Archibald—tea, with my aunt. But we can go out this morning to see what can be found."

He looked appalled. "You're leaving me alone at this crucial juncture? You choose *now* not to hold up your part of the bargain? 'Frailty, thy name is Woman!'" said he. The man who had locked himself in his bedroom for a full day.

"I give you full marks for the Shakespeare," replied I. "Alas, it cannot be helped. Lady Spencer, as you know, is implacable."

Archibald wiped his hand across his face in defeat. "I expect you to come up with something before you go," stated he. "You are, as always, an utter disappointment."

Unnecessarily, thought I.

Later

Well.

Tea was amusing for Arabella, at very least.

I was welcomed into the First drawing room—a good sign. Aunt Eugenia was there, sitting at a small writing desk.

"Ah, Emma. There you are. Still pinched, even though I've given you a week or more of rest."

"Yes, Aunt."

The tea arrived, my aunt ordered me to prepare two cups, and then she came over and sniffed. "Not very well done, but what can one expect? Now, have you assembled a list of your worst qualities? I'm assuming you've written them out, seeing how they are extensive."

I admitted I had not.

She *tsked*.

It was then that Arabella floated into the room. I offered her a rueful expression, and she, eyes laughing, sat down across from me. "I hear we are discussing your faults today, Emma."

"It seems so."

"The purpose of this exercise," Aunt Eugenia stated, "is to root out those we have no use for, and support that which makes Arabella shine. I will suggest the first. You look like you know too much. It does not serve you, nor Arabella. What can be done?"

I opened my mouth, then closed it. Glancing towards Arabella, who leaned back in full enjoyment, I said, "I thought my shoddy education took care of any such worries, Aunt. I assure you, there are a great many things I do not know."

Aunt Eugenia looked towards heaven as if to gather strength from God Almighty. "*I* know how Ignorant you are. The problem is, you don't look it! And your vocabulary is a good twenty percent more intelligent than it should be. What do you suggest we do?"

"I could repeat the more banal words in my arsenal…?" I suggested.

"Fine, fine. Which?"

I slouched. "Which words?"

"Yes, provide for me an example. And don't slouch."

I faltered a moment and then put effort into sounding simple. "Oh, Lord West, I find rain to be a repeated thing in a country that has a lot of rain. Don't you agree?"

Arabella clapped, and I gave her a threatening glare.

"Good," Aunt Eugenia said, preparing herself another cup of tea. "Simple, repetitive, inane. Now, what are we going to do about your eye rolling?"

The entire tea proceeded *like so*.

I was allowed to keep my face—thankfully, for I wonder just what her alternative would be?—also, my past.

"Arabella taking pity on an orphaned cousin reflects well on her. Tell as many people as you like how alone and poor you are."

(If she only knew. I've sworn Arabella to secrecy regarding my loss of funds.)

I may also keep my table manners, and my smile—as long as I do not use it too often, yet it must be ready when Aunt Eugenia so mandates. "You are to be content, but not particularly happy for the next fortnight. I want you to be an object of pity. It will reflect well on Arabella, who has, to put it frankly, everything you do and everything you do not."

I find my ability to laugh at Aunt Eugenia's insults relatively robust, but even my great talent was taxed by the time she released me back into the wild.

July 7th

I've done it! I have figured out the first clue.

England is mine! The entire United Kingdom is mine! St. Crispian's at the very least. Or possibly just my garret? But the victorious sentiment holds.

This morning I went to Everett's and selected a box of pastries for moral support after yesterday's assassination of my character. My banker, Mr. Penury, might not have approved of the full half-dozen I purchased, but desperate times and all that.

And then, on my walk back up Whereabouts towards home, I was nearly knocked flat by a gang of boys running across the street and slipping through a hole in the fence to my left. They whooped like banshees, filthy and happy to be so. After the threat had passed, I continued, only to pause mid-step. Boys. Marbles. Boys play marbles, boys who run in gangs through the streets and know where loose boards in fences live. Stepping back, I eyed the fence and then the street, and finding myself unobserved, I pushed the board aside and followed.

It was an overgrown half alley between two fences that opened up into a small worn patch of dirt. It was there I found the boys holding court.

Agnes is calling up the stairs. (Her mother would not approve.)

I wonder what she needs.

Later

Agnes wanted to tell me a joke. A joke!

I stood patiently as she prepared herself and asked the question.

"What do you call a woman without a hat?"

After some attempt, I said, "I've no idea. What?"

Then, as she was about to respond, her face went blank.

"Miss Lion!" She clapped her hands over her mouth. "I've forgotten!"

"We can't win all our battles," I smiled, in an effort to appease.

Now. Where was I?

Oh yes. I'd found the boys in the alleyway.

The leader—who I guessed to be the leader for having claimed the only branch on a half cut-down tree—had one leg on the branch, the other swinging wildly.

They stared.

I was a very unwelcome guest.

My instinct in dealing with this tribe of unfriendly natives was not to speak gibberish and risk misunderstanding. Instead, I decided to barter. Fishing the marble out of my pocket, I held it up to the light—it really was a lovely green—and then tossed it to the boy watching from the tree.

He caught it with one hand, rolled it between two fingers, then gave a quick jerk of his head to one of the boys below him on the ground. The young lad with a cap askew on his head fished around in his pocket as he walked towards me, then brought his hand into a fist. Understanding the language, I held out my gloved hand and waited.

He dropped a silver coin into my palm.

Instead of staring at it—no, I was in too world-wise company for that—I slipped it into my pocket, handed over the box of pastries as thanks, tipped my hat, and disappeared back out the alley and through the fence.

Very prettily done.

Later

Cousin Archibald and I held a conclave over dinner this evening regarding the meaning of the coin. (No relatives were harmed, I almost regret to say.) It is no coinage of England, with a silhouette of Caesar on one side and a silhouette of whom I suppose to be Brutus on the other. Around Caesar's head it reads, "Et Tu, Brute?"—the famed last words of our dear Julius.

It is quite a lovely little thing, and if it weren't a clue, I would have it made into a necklace.

Cousin Archibald was beside himself with the mystery of the coin. I had to tell how it came into my possession three times. He was upset there were children involved. Cousin Archibald dislikes children on principle.

After wading through the mess of words Cousin Archibald spewed as he insisted THERE MUST BE ANOTHER MESSAGE STAMPED INTO THE COIN, I took a more practical bent.

"What can one do with a coin?" I posited. "One can buy something with it. Or throw it in a fountain for luck."

We sat for a moment, looked at each other, then shouted, "Baron's Square!"

A rare moment of parallel thought.

For Baron's Square boasts the only fountain in all of St. Crispian's.

It is a replication of Cellini's famed statue of Perseus holding the head of Medusa; tragic, grotesque, and strangely moving, seeing as how our version was designed so the water falls from Medusa's closed eyes. It is heartbreaking. One does not cheer on the victor as much as one marvels over the weeping head of the woman gripped in Perseus's hand.

Archibald and I decided that the fountain merited immediate investigation.

"I dislike all this being seen with you in public," he said with fervour.

"Lucky for both of us, it is dark," I replied.

Gathering our necessary accoutrements, we left Lapis Lazuli House in the cover of said darkness and made our way up to Baron's Square.

No one else was at the fountain. Given the hour, it was no surprise.

We walked around it, peered into the water to see if any of the coins matched our particular specimen, and Archibald only spat out three insults.

He, having rolled up the sleeve of his coat—instead of removing it as someone who was really a person would—occupied himself by plunging his hand in for fistfuls of coins.

I, on the other hand, began to study Perseus and our weeping Medusa.

It is grotesque in many ways, Perseus standing atop Medusa's decapitated body, and what a job he made of it, as the sight of her neck *not* having been a clean cut has always given me a chill up my spine. However, I cannot deny it was well done.

I've always remembered what my father said about the story.

It makes me feel a bit sad.

It was in that moment that I realised Archibald was *taking* the fountain coins and stuffing them in his pockets. He will bring down every curse upon us, I swear it.

"Cousin Archibald! What are you doing?" demanded I.

"Looking for clues," snapped he.

"You cannot steal other people's wishes! It's the worst sort of luck. Put them back!"

If someone had overheard what we were saying, they would have thought us both lunatics.

"It's clearly telling us to look to the power of man," insisted he.

"Perseus was a demigod. Don't flatter yourself," came my swift rejoinder.

It cast us both into momentary silence.

He suggested we think of Medusa's head, as killing her was the focus of his mission. It did not sit well with me.

"No, the deed is done; there is power in it no longer," I answered. "We are here to take action, so we must think of the action. The action, the sword? The sword points downward until the edge, which takes a wicked curve upward and..." We both followed the line of the point and found ourselves staring directly at a second floor window of General Braithwaite's house.

(The rumour is that only the general would buy the house directly in front of the fountain. No one else could bear the weeping.)

It seemed a rather far-fetched idea that the sword pointed us to our clue until, at the very window we were staring at, there came a rustle of curtain and a bit of light. A candle revealed then concealed, three times.

I started to walk towards it.

"Where are you going?" cried Archibald.

"It is our sign, Cousin."

"It is to trick us!"

I believe I said something encouraging, such as, "Don't be an imbecile!"

We knocked on General Braithwaite's door after I'd made certain Cousin Archibald had put back every coin in…

July 8th

I fell asleep last night at my desk, only to wake in the deep hours of morning—I believe it was to the sound of Mr. Pierce coming up his stairs—and I have such a sore neck. It will be difficult to keep my head up for Young Hawkes's sermon.

I flipped through the last several days of my journal and am appalled and amused how much time it takes to get it all down. I've gone to sleep late every night, which won't do next week as I've several obligations to fulfil for Aunt Eugenia.

It may be Emma M. Lion who is found dead on the fifteenth, not Caesar.

The events at General Braithwaite's last night are cloudy. I remember hearing more about the supply line of Her Majesty's Armed Forces than I ever thought I would, and I recall the General telling us to keep hold of our coin and remember the number—oh dear. Was it seventy-one? I believe it was.

He then berated us for being out of our barracks at such a time and sent us packing. It may be too wonderful to be fact, but I seem to recall the general poking Cousin Archibald's posterior with the point of his sword on our way out.

Delightful, if true.

Later

Young Hawkes delivered a short, somewhat weary sermon on the blind leading the blind—biblical and a *Julius Caesar* reference—after which he closed the Bible with a snap, looked out at all of us, and stated quite plainly, "Let it be known that I know nothing in regards to *Julius Caesar*, and will no longer entertain communications on the subject. If there is a death in your family, you are welcome to contact me; otherwise, I will see you all next Sunday. Amen."

There was no hymn.

And instead of waiting to shake hands with any of the parishioners, he walked out the doors, across the street, and—if the witnesses are reliable—straight into The Cleopatra.

Well.

July 9th

As Agnes was ironing my petticoat this morning, she said, "My mother once said that if Brutus had been a Scot, he never would-a been found out for the murder of Julius Caesar."

"Hmm, I'm sure," I answered, half-distracted by sewing an errant button onto my dress. "Although, if Brutus had been a Scot, he would not have been in a position to murder anyone on the floor of the Roman Senate, Caesar or otherwise."

Agnes screwed up her nose and gave what I'd said real consideration.

Later

Yesterday, I utterly refused to follow our clue—it *is* the number seventy-one, as a torn piece of paper testified in my weary handwriting—and begged off in the name of the Sabbath.

"I will be in church, Cousin Archibald, and then I intend to spend the remainder of the day in a solemn introspection of my own soul," stated I.

"Do not get lost in the black mire you will find there," snarled he.

I felt his comment was rather pot-and-kettle.

Today, having been refreshed by my journey into the black mire that is Emma M. Lion, I went downstairs after breakfast, ready for battle.

To my slight disappointment, Cousin Archibald was waiting, his brows as beetled as any villain's.

A lesser mortal might have hoped he would have passed quietly in the night.

I, however, would have settled for him passing rather loudly.

Together, in actuality if not in spirit, Cousin Archibald and I walked every street in St. Crispian's.

Having seen nothing else, we reasoned the seventy-one referenced a house number. There was such a house number on both Traitors

Road and the Diagonal. We began with Traitors.

Cousin Archibald, who refused, and I quote, "to risk the acquisition of fleas," stayed on the sidewalk while I went up the steps and used the brass knocker to make my presence known. It took three attempts before there was an answer.

"Yes'm?" said the man who opened the door.

"I've reason to believe you might have something for me."

He blinked a time or two, looked rather harried, then said, "Is that man part of your search?"

I looked over my shoulder at Cousin Archibald standing beside the street, batting away a fly that kept trying to assault his face. "He is," I admitted reluctantly. "However unfortunate."

"All right then. Come in."

I followed him into a darkly painted hall where he stopped at a bowl on the side table.

"I've been instructed to give you this." And he handed me a slip of paper.

It had a picture of the sun on it, with the words, "*Theā Philopátōra*."

"Is this all?" I asked. "Is there any other message?"

"No other message."

"Any idea what it means?"

"No idea, Miss."

I thanked him, regardless, and left.

Archibald took the clue from my hand as soon as he was able and read it aloud. Then the blood drained from his face, and he said, "Curse this perverse game."

I asked him if he knew the meaning of the clue.

"How should I!" After that pronouncement, he wiped the back of his hand beneath his nose and turned, walking down Traitors Road without me.

Theā Philopátōra?

July 10th

YOU WERE SPEAKING IN EARNEST WHEN YOU SAID I WOULD ENCOUNTER QUOTES FROM JULIUS CAESAR.

Of course! What happened?

I WENT TO THE REED AND RITE TO SEE IF I HAD ANY MISPLACED ITEMS IN THE KEEP, AS ABSURD AS THAT ENTIRE SCHEME IS.

WHILE THERE, I HAD A CUP OF COFFEE AND SOMETHING TO EAT.

A FEW MEN WERE AT THE COUNTER LAUGHING AT WHO KNOWS WHAT. ONE OF THEM POINTED AND SAID, "YOND CASSIUS HAS A LEAN AND HUNGRY LOOK; HE THINKS TOO MUCH: SUCH MEN ARE DANGEROUS."

IT WAS FOLLOWED WITH LAUGHTER, AND A CHEER.

You were called out as Cassius? How infamous, Mr. Pierce.

HAVE I DONE SOMETHING TO EARN SUCH PUBLIC IRE?

It is simply the old guard having a bit of fun at the expense of a new denizen. It's a form of welcome.

IS IT? I CERTAINLY DID NOT FEEL WELCOME, SITTING WITH HALF A GINGER CAKE IN MY MOUTH, LOOKING AN ABSOLUTE FOOL.

Oh no! Certainly not, Mr. Pierce. Had you looked a fool, they would have used a different quote from the play. To be shouted the 'Yond Cassius' line is an honour of sorts. A backwards compliment. It happened to my father once.

THIS IS THE MOST RIDICULOUS PLACE I HAVE EVER LIVED.

Isn't it? Why we love it, I suppose.

Did you find anything belonging to you in The Keep?

A PAIR OF SOCKS.

Here's to the small victories.

July 11th

Just received a line from Roland. Having not seen hide nor hair of him for almost a fortnight, I found I've missed him. Oh, how the dastardly deeds of childhood fade.

Emma,

Spending a few weeks with a chum in the country. Pleasant, as London's been uncomfortably warm. Do you remember how I (we) promised Miss Hunt and her brother an opera? (However mercenary her intentions may or may not be.) I have begged her forgiveness, casting my escape in terms of a personal emergency, with a vow to fulfil my promise in August when The Magic Flute *begins its run. Seeing as how you are partially responsible for bringing me unto this web of deceit, I expect you to attend with bells on.*

Would you like me to send anything? A bit of country sun? A small wood? A running brook? A flower?

Your Obedient Servant,
Roland Sutherland

Roland,

You are a goat. Had your childhood self read such a display of poetry, he would have dug a hole and placed you inside. As for The Magic Flute, *I've never seen it and have always wished to. I will accompany you and the Hunts. (You did ask for my help, I remind you.) I suggest we recruit Arabella. If your desire—and it may not be?—is to disinterest Miss Hunt, then Arabella's mere presence will strike fear into her mercenary heart. August it is.*

Regarding your proposed gifts: As I've not the space in my garret for a wood or a brook, however lovely the idea, I would be happy to receive a flower from your travels. Beware, while I do not have a copy of Floral Emblems *or* Language of Flowers, *I have read them both. And therefore, if you send me a Bay Rhododendron or a Birdsfoot Trefoil, I will know you are wishing me an early grave. If you send me a Wild Tansy, war it is.*

Emma

I'm off now to attend a dinner with Aunt Eugenia and Arabella. That is, if Cousin Archibald doesn't slay me before I've gone out the door. He's very upset that I've not sorted out our clue. Well, I haven't. Last night I attended a dinner I expected to be trying that was actually agreeable. Something I did not expect. (I blame that universal imbalance on Archibald Flat.) If he wants to run around screaming "*Theā Philopátōra?*" to any who will listen, all the power in the world to him.

I am going to dine, with the expectation of some very fine food.

Later

The food was fine, but the meal dragged on so long a dowager fainted between courses from fatigue.

I was quite cheered by this unexpected gift.

A little hubbub in the dining room is rarely amiss.

Arabella and I were able to find an uninterrupted corner after we women quitted the men. Enough time for private conversation. After giving Arabella a brief synopsis of the *Julius Caesar* saga, telling of the chase from clue to clue with grand dramatics, I said I was stumped with the last clue in my possession.

"What is it?"

I slipped the paper out of my glove—for of course one would

carry a cryptic message in her glove at a dinner party—and handed it to Arabella.

"*Theā Philopátōra*," I spoke aloud as she considered the phrase. "I suppose I need to find myself a library and a book on Greek."

Arabella flushed, an unusual occurrence, and held the paper up between her two fingers. "Oh Emma, you should have come to me sooner. I know what this means."

"You?" I asked rather pointedly.

"Me," Arabella drawled. "Many think I'm just a pretty face, but you know better, dear Cousin. *Theā Philopátōra* means 'goddess who loves her father.'"

I did not believe her.

"Don't expect me to be fooled by your perverse sense of humour, Arabella."

Arabella scoffed—well, as much as she is able while maintaining a completely languid yet pleasurable expression. "Disbelieve me if you will, Emma, but *Theā Philopátōra* means 'goddess who loves her father.'"

"And how would you know that?" I challenged. "You're no master of Greek."

Then Arabella looked like she had a meaningful thought behind her eyes. "Because it is what my father called me. *Theā Philopátōra*. It is one of the names of she whose other name was 'glory to her father,' also known as Cleopatra. There. Does that mean anything to you?"

Arabella does not invoke the memory of her father lightly, but I still said, "Are you teasing me?"

"No," she replied. "Why?"

"Because The Cleopatra is the name of St. Crispian's pub."

"Well then, I've sorted your clue for you. Now, as fascinated as I am with dead emperors—which is not very—I would much rather hear how your Tenant fares."

When Arabella lifts two eyebrows, it is to let you know you've done something silly. When she raises one, it is to let you know you're doing something interesting.

She raised only the one.

And seeing as how she had sorted my clue for me, I decided to lay an offering on the altar of the goddess. "I believe The Tenant fares well. I like him, what I know of him that is. If you promise secrecy, I will tell you that I've agreed to let the salon to him, to use as a portrait studio. It's to help supplement my income."

"Emma! How cunning of you, and wholly inappropriate under the right circumstances."

"Not so!" It was too robust a defence, for Aunt Eugenia glared at the two of us before returning to her conversation. I leaned forward and with a lowered voice said, "He's installing a door to Lapis Lazuli Minor, and will enter and leave from there. It will, in essence, become a part of his rooms."

"And the door that leads into your hall?"

"Will remain respectfully shut a good deal of the time, I imagine."

"You are merging living spaces?"

"It isn't like that!"

Arabella's slow smile disagreed. "A man a few years past thirty, Emma. You are a scandal! What does he look like then? Hold nothing back. I want an artist's description. Considering you drank port with the man, he cannot be ugly."

"Flawed logic," I replied under my breath. "Very well. In all honesty, I consider him very handsome. He is no Apollo, like Roland, rather another metal entirely. His features are sharp. His hair is dark, a touch longer than the current fashion. Clean shaven—no mustache, thank the Fates that be. His eyes, well, I'm always trying to catch just what they are: silver most days and storm cloud all the rest."

Arabella settled further into her seat, half concealing her smile. "Go on."

"I don't sit and *stare* at the man, Arabella. There isn't a good deal more to say."

"He sounds like an avenging angel."

And there it was. Arabella had spoken the words that fit Mr. Pierce with almost terrifying accuracy.

"Avenging Angel," I repeated. "Perhaps he is. There is a potency about his person, and I can't decipher if it's like the tremor just before the storm or the uncertain relief after it's broken. Fear? Or awe? He certainly occupies a room like no other man I've met."

"Emma dear?"

"Yes?"

"I will only say this once—"

And that was the moment Aunt Eugenia called us both over, the *tête-à-tête* cut short. We graciously joined the party just as the men did and were not left alone again.

At the end of the night, Aunt Eugenia and Arabella saw me to the door, where a carriage waited on the street to take me home. The reason for my aunt's attention was to enquire after my nonexistent chaperone.

"Does she feel terribly bad to be excluded, Emma?"

"She's delighted for me, Aunt, however she would feel awkward at a dinner or in a ballroom. She's content to wait at home."

"How unfortunate. It's always best to strike envy in the hearts of one's servants. It keeps them easy to manipulate. You must foster such feelings, Emma."

"Yes, Aunt."

I left feeling far more scandalous than when I had arrived.

*July 12th*

I don't feel that what happened at The Cleopatra was entirely my fault.

Some may argue ~~otherwise~~ that it remains to be seen.

A Subjective View of the Day
by Emma M. Lion

When I informed Cousin Archibald that the clue led us to The Cleopatra, I fully expected him to take the reins, seeing as how I had never entered the pub, dear to the male inhabitants of our neighbourhood. While St. Crispian's gives great allowance to peculiarities, and the harsh lens of social criticism is rose-coloured to the extreme, there are still certain attitudes tied to the female gender and the Appropriate Place thereof. As a woman, I am certainly at greater liberty to take liberties, as it were; however, there is one place where such progressive notions are not wanted: The Cleopatra. The only woman wanted in The Cleopatra is Cleopatra herself, represented by a statue near the front door that the bachelors drape with cheap jewellery for luck.

When I suggested Cousin Archibald go and enjoy a pint while rustling up a clue—that particular choice of words making me think of Archibald as an American cattleman, a worthwhile entertainment for any dull day—he looked apprehensive.

And then panicked.

And then he attempted to loosen his collar.

Something was terribly wrong.

"Cousin," said I, "have you aught to say?"

"I cannot," croaked he, "I cannot go to The Cleopatra."

"Whyever not?" quizzed I.

"They banished me. I am banned absolutely. Until the end of time."

"For what!"

"It was long ago. I've no desire to reimagine the spiteful experience."

As much as I wished to press for the story, I frowned instead and placed my hands on my hips in a way that reminded me of my mother. "Then we are in such a pickle."

Cousin Archibald, for once, looked almost as if he were considering a contrite sentiment.

"We could send Parian," was his suggestion, after which he cleared his throat.

"That won't do. I shall go."

"And do what?" demanded he.

"Order a pint, if I must."

It was then that he snorted. "Nothing is sacred to your kind."

"My kind?" Was he again attacking my generation as a whole?

Alas, no.

"Womenkind. The Curse of Adam. The Weaker Sex."

It was in that moment I pulled my mouth to one side and looked pointedly towards The Scar.

Needless to say, as I gathered my things, pinned my errant locks, and left the house, he was still yelling his opinions regarding My Degenerate State and Adam's Rib.

The walk to The Cleopatra did not last nearly as long as I thought it should have. Sooner than I liked, I was standing on the corner of Traitors and the Diagonal, and there she was, St. Crispian's beloved Egyptian queen.

"This is for Julius," I muttered to myself, before squaring my shoulders and opening the door.

It was a slightly dim room, and I noted a burdened Cleopatra to my right, covered in paste jewels, baubles, and beads. She did not look particularly pleased. I gave the wooden figure a look of commiseration.

It wasn't until I took a few steps towards the counter that the hum of midday male voices shifted to a lower start and stop. They had identified a female in their midst.

Some did not appear to think anything of it. Others were not pleased to see me.

The barkeep was wiping down glasses, and it took stepping up to the counter between two men and clearing my throat for him to look up.

"You lost, Miss?"

"Um, no, actually. I'm looking for…"

And it was with a great smirk that he suggested, "A pint?"

Before I could gather my thoughts to ask after the clue, I said, "That would be lovely. I'll be at that table over there."

I didn't want a pint, let alone a table.

One of the men seated nearby laughed.

I could have pointed out there was food in his teeth. I didn't.

However tempted I might have been.

My mother raised me to be better than that.

More's the pity.

Seeing I was committed to the visual of a pint—at very least—I turned heel and stepped towards a booth against the back wall. It would have been far more impressive had a man not been standing on my skirt.

The rip of my hem only drew more attention.

"Pardon me, *Miss*," said the perpetrator of the crime.

Another man nearby said, "Steady on, fellow. Give the miss some room."

Gathering all my Irish pride, I turned towards the culprit, and instead of a gracious reply, I simply made the sound of, "Hmm."

Then I took my seat facing the room. I thought of the card Young Hawkes had given me those years ago. Undaunted, it said.

So undaunted I sat.

Many stared anyway.

It was demoralizing to find the average state of our society tucked inside my lovely, exceptional St. Crispian's. It must be owned, however, that not *all* of the men were bothered by my presence. Mr. Hathaway, a neighbour on Whereabouts, lifted a hand and smiled in my direction. I smiled back.

When the pint was brought, it was slammed down so as to slosh half of it on the table—which was fine by me. I had no intention of drinking much of anything so early in the day.

But the barkeep stood there, crossing his arms as if to call my bluff.

What this man did not know was that I battled the great Lady Eugenia Spencer on a weekly basis and had lived with Cousin Matilde for three gruelling years. He did not scare me.

I gripped the handle of the large glass and took a drink.

When I set it back on the table, I said, "Decent. I've had better."

It was then that the barkeep threw back his head and started laughing.

A thing I did not enjoy, as every pair of eyes looked towards us.

"Anything else I can bring you? A hard cider, perhaps? Or something foreign enough to burn your innards right up? After you've finished your pint, of course."

Just as I opened my mouth, it was filled with someone else's voice.

"Gibbs, I see you've been welcoming my guest. Would you bring me a lemonade? Miss Lion? Would you like one as well to go with your…pint?"

I was looking up at the face of Young Hawkes, in the flesh.

"Lemonade would be just fine," I replied.

Gibbs looked immediately contrite, reclaiming the pint. "Hawkes. I didn't realise— I'm sorry that—" Hawkes gave him a long look as Gibbs finished with, "I'll see to you and the young miss here."

"Splendid," Hawkes answered. "The table appears to need some attention. Would you—?"

And before Hawkes could say anything else, Gibbs had wiped down the table and hurried away after our tame lemonades.

Hawkes did not speak immediately, settling across from me, his hair askew, blue eyes giving nothing away. When the attention of the room went back to its familiar hum and we could not be overheard, he said, "Miss Lion."

"Young Hawkes."

"Have you turned to midday drinking?"

Heavens no, I thought. Though if Cousin Archibald were to drive one to a vice, that would certainly be it.

"I ordered the pint by mistake. Although I'm deep in the appearance of evil, aren't I?"

Hawkes simply looked at me a moment, and then, "Appearance of mischief is more apropos for one Emma Lion. Your cousin might argue evil, however."

"Oh dear." I believe I inserted a sigh at that juncture. "Have you been hearing his confessions again?"

"I've limited him to ten complaints in relation to your person each visit."

I could strangle Cousin Archibald.

"Only ten? How very limiting. What has he had to say about my sins?"

Looking away from me, Young Hawkes tapped his hand on the table as if it were an instrument. "That would be deemed confidential, even if you did assault Mr. Flat with a sword."

He could *not* have been serious.

"That was not I. It was General Braithwaite!"

Finally, Hawkes's habitual and somewhat pained philosophical expression broke for a smile. "Pity. I was rather impressed with your swashbuckling potential."

"Well, I never said I lacked swashbuckling potential."

I think most of the events of my life have pointed towards piracy of some sort.

This I did not add.

Young Hawkes knows too much already.

Gibbs returned, glasses of lemonade delivered with a very congenial invitation for Hawkes to ask for anything else he'd like, on the house.

"No, no. Thank you, Gibbs. Miss Lion is an especial friend of mine, and I'm pleased your establishment has taken so good care."

I covered my snort with a rather convincing cough, and Gibbs had the good grace to look ashamed. "Only the best for your friends, Young Hawkes. Isn't that right, boys?" he yelled out to the rest of the pub. A cheer of agreement ran through the men like a hobbled horse—how enthusiastic is that?—but it does seem Hawkes carries real credit at The Cleopatra.

After Gibbs left us alone, I turned to my blessed lemonade and thanked Young Hawkes, telling him I hadn't had anything to eat for hours and was not looking forward to a pint on an empty stomach.

"Pardon the question, Miss Lion, but why *are* you here for a pint on an empty stomach? I did not think you frequented The Cleopatra."

"This is the proverbial First," I answered. "And I would tell you why I'm here, but you specifically requested in your Sunday sermon that we not speak to you of *Julius Caesar*."

"So that's it. What is this clue you are chasing?"

I withdrew the silver coin from my reticule and set it on the table between us.

Hawkes picked it up and studied one side, then the other.

He asked if I had shown it to Gibbs.

I answered, no, I had not.

He then called Gibbs over and showed the man my coin. "This belongs to Miss Lion. Do you have anything for her?"

Gibbs flushed. "I do, but…"

"I need it, Gibbs," I answered for myself. "It is why I am here."

The barkeep looked at me a long moment, as if he were the harbinger of my destruction. "Very well, Miss Lion. It isn't a pint you need. Or a lemonade. You've ordered for yourself a Cleopatra."

Hawkes, spiritual guide and religious leader, closed his eyes and made a sound of disbelief. He muttered something that sounded like, "Only Emma Lion would…" but I cannot be sure.

"What is a Cleopatra?"

The man did not answer.

Young Hawkes pursed his lips, then asked, "Is a Cleopatra necessary, Gibbs?"

"I don't make the rules, Hawkes. And rules is rules. Had she found the other clues, she would be chasing a different path, but those are the ones she found, so here she is. Bearing in mind, I think this clue was meant for a gentleman."

It was a moment of great insight.

First, I had no idea there was more than one road that led to Rome.

Second, different clues were given to gentlemen and ladies. Or so it seems. The man who gave me the clue for The Cleopatra must have thought it would be Cousin Archibald attending.

Curious.

After Gibbs left to procure what I assumed would be my ruination, I asked Young Hawkes, "Is the Cleopatra so bad?"

He did not answer, saying nothing until Gibbs returned a few minutes later, setting a glass in front of me with what looked like black pitch from the street.

"What in heaven's name is that?"

"The Cleopatra, Miss."

"Oh dear."

"I don't make the rules," he repeated somewhat defensively.

I stared at the concoction half a moment, then braced myself.

"Any last words before my impending doom?" I asked Young Hawkes.

"Would you like your final rites?"

Ominous.

"If you've a blessing for me, Hawkes," I said, picking up the glass, "now is the time."

He sighed. "Miss Lion, I bless you to slay the dragon."

"Amen," muttered Gibbs, and it was followed by several other amens, at which point I realised every eye in the room was on me.

I pinched my lips, cursed my empty stomach, and with a prayer that sounded remarkably like a whimper, downed the Cleopatra in one, sludgy swallow.

It was death in a glass. Misery and gutter, followed by a kick of pepper, black liquorice, and who knows what else. It almost didn't stay down. Twice my stomach revolted, and as I fought to hold the Cleopatra in her place, everyone took a quick intake of breath.

Except Hawkes. He watched intently, with unwavering focus.

It was a strange comfort to have the clergy be one's second in such a venture.

When I knew I had won, I slammed the glass on the table to a round of applause.

I could not read Hawkes's expression—mostly for having my eyes closed as I swore I would never eat or drink anything ever again—but it was he who told Gibbs, "If you've anything for Miss Lion, bring it now. It's time we two be on our way."

Gibbs handed over a card, which Hawkes slipped into his coat pocket, and he stood, coming around to help me up.

I thought I managed rather well, walking with my chin up, blurry eyes focused on the door. Hawkes's supporting hand on my elbow may have helped.

Once we were out in bright daylight—too bright—Hawkes asked how I was feeling.

"I think I've been trammelled by a train."

"You have. The Cleopatra is meant to put full grown men under the table, and it has. Home with you. I'll see you to Lapis Lazuli House myself. Do you have any obligations this evening?"

"A card party with my aunt."

"Cry off. Send a note round saying you've a headache."

"I'm not sure I've a head possible of aching, Young Hawkes," I replied. "I think it's gone."

His expression was all sympathy, even if he did lift a finger and poke my forehead to prove that I did, indeed, still have a head.

"My aunt will brook no excuses."

"I will write the letter. Come along. Put your arm through mine and mind the uneven walk along the Diagonal. Let's not add insult to injury."

It felt ages until we were walking up the steps of Lapis Lazuli House. Hawkes went right through the front door and called to Agnes, who came running from the kitchen.

"Is she dead!" she cried, when she saw me clinging to his arm.

"Certainly not, Agnes! I'm standing on my own two feet," I hissed.

"Of sorts, Miss Lion."

We went into the drawing room where Young Hawkes was so good as to see me to the green sofa. I slumped against the arm while he rattled off a list of something or other to Agnes. It made no sense to my muddled mind.

Agnes left, and Hawkes sat across from me in the pink chair, running a hand through his errant hair. We waited in silence until Agnes returned, stirring something foul looking in a glass.

"I think I remembered everything you told me," Agnes told Young Hawkes.

"Thank you. Now, Miss Lion, I do apologise, but if you want to be on your feet tomorrow, I would drink this now."

"You are a villain," I muttered. After a small eternity of thinking the theatrical society of St. Crispian's was a dastardly organization, I finally sat up and accepted the poison.

I could only drink half—it was almost as bad as the Cleopatra—but once Young Hawkes deemed I'd had enough, he set it on the table and suggested Agnes help me to my rooms.

"I've got to write Aunt Eugenia."

"I'll write the letter, and Agnes can help me with the direction."

I cannot remember if I said goodbye or not, but Agnes supported me up the stairs, and I fell asleep before I was on my bed. I woke a quarter to midnight, feeling remarkably well, considering, only to find a peach envelope waiting on my desk.

I've been avoiding it, but I suppose I should read it now.

> *Dearest Emma,*
>
> *I am sorry to hear of your being indisposed after the great service you gave to your parish. I was happy to make your excuses for this evening, but hope you are well enough to join us tomorrow.*
>
> *Your Aunt*

I've just blinked several times, washed my face, and read it twice over. It sounds nothing like Aunt Eugenia. What on earth did Young Hawkes write?

Do vicars lie…?

Oh dear. I think I ought to go back to bed.

July 13th

I cannot make it out. The clue, a card Young Hawkes left, is a simple line drawing of a bird. Its meaning obscured to my mind.

Archibald the Coward and I have again traipsed St. Crispian's all the day long. Nothing. *Nothing.* Save a near altercation with my elderly cousin, and an hour later a man stopping to applaud me in the street.

I did not explain why.

Now I must change for dinner at Spencer House.

Later

Just returned from dinner at Aunt Eugenia's—"*Emma dear, what remarkable service you've rendered your parish; now see if you can manage some mediocre aid on my and Arabella's behalf.*"

(Bless Hawkes.)

I've mused on the clue all evening. No enlightenment whatsoever.

Perhaps I ought to pace.

YOU'VE BEEN AWAKE FOR HOURS.

I thought you were asleep. Have I kept you up?

NO. I'VE BEEN AWAKE.

I have a clue I cannot figure. And Julius Caesar *is on Sunday night. The final tickets are given on the fourteenth, which is tomorrow. I'm hours away from my destruction.*

AT WHOSE HAND?

The options are many.

WHAT'S THE CLUE?

A card with a line drawing of a bird.

DO BIRDS HOLD SIGNIFICANCE IN ST. CRISPIAN'S?

Not that I know.

SEND THE CARD THROUGH.

THAT ISN'T A BIRD. IT'S A GLOVE.

It's not a glove. It's a bird. Turn the card round.

INTERESTING. IT'S A BIRD FROM ONE VIEW, A GLOVE FROM THE OTHER. LOOK FOR YOURSELF.

You're right! Any thoughts as to what the glove means?

DO YOU KNOW THE GENTLEMAN'S SHOP ON KING HENRY'S ROAD, DOWN THE CORNER AND LEFT FROM WHEREABOUTS? IT'S CALLED THE HOUND.

I've seen it, yes.

THEY SELL QUALITY GLOVES, AND THE CIRCLE THAT IS EITHER THE BIRD'S EYE, OR A BUTTON ON THE GLOVE, BEARS THEIR MARK.

Bless you, Mr. Pierce! I'll go first thing.

TELL CHAMBERS I SAID HELLO.

Oh dear. Not The Pirate.

THE VERY SAME.

GOODNIGHT

Goodnight

July 14th

This morning I sent a dour-faced Parian to inform Cousin Archibald that I'd solved the clue.

Parian sniffed and informed me that Cousin Archibald had gone out.

"Out?" I said.

"Out."

"Out to find a clue? Or out to some other place?"

"Simply out, Miss Lion. I know nothing more."

I did not believe him, though I couldn't deny I preferred going to The Hound alone. Upon entering the shop, I found that I was the only customer. Having braced myself for The Pirate, it was a relief to see a school-aged young man behind the counter.

"Good morning," he said. "Would you like to buy a gift for your husband?"

To which I answered, "What a lovely idea. What would you recommend?"

"As you can see, we have cigarette cases, custom leather-bound books, gloves, scarves, a gold-plated shaving kit…"

"Heavens. When I find him, *if* I find him, I'll return with the express purpose of purchasing one of your fine products."

The young man looked perplexed. "Have you lost him, Miss?"

I did not mean for my humour to turn dark. "I've lost one young man, yes. As for a second, well, I sometimes doubt his existence." Receiving no answer, I took the card out of my reticule and placed it on the counter. "Today I am only here about this."

"Ahh." He was thankful for the change in subject. "One or two?"

"One or two what?"

"Tickets."

"It's over then? What a relief. I'll take two."

And the young man opened a drawer, withdrew two red tickets, and handed them to me.

There are times in one's life when one knows they are exactly where they are meant to be, and a chorus of angels in the expanse of eternity cheers.

This was one of those moments.

The Great Shakespearean Tragedy
JULIUS CAESAR
July 15th 1883

Flipping the ticket over, I saw an address (On Sterling Street), an assigned time to arrive (8:13), and a threat of immediate ruin if information is shared with any living soul.

What joy!

I'm now home and have told Parian to send Cousin Archibald up to my garret once he shows his face.

I'm relieved to have our fraught partnership almost at an end.

Now I've nothing to do but wait.

It's warm. Even for July.

I believe I will open both garret doors and try to coax a cross-breeze.

Later

It has been a day ordained by the Fates, for how else could one explain the wholly cursed chain of events?

I certainly cannot.

It was nearing midday when I was startled by the sudden appearance of Cousin Archibald in the garret doorway. I was sitting at the window reading.

"Lazy wastrel," he sniffed, his forehead marked with sweat. "Have you figured out the clue?"

Lazy wastrel? The man wants for a mirror.

I gave him an evil eye—rather Greek of me—then shut Father's *Shakespeare* and left it on the window seat. Sitting at my desk, I opened the drawer and retrieved one of the red tickets.

"I've not only figured out the clue, Cousin, I've secured us each a ticket. As agreed, however undeserving, here is yours."

I held it out.

A change overtook Cousin Archibald. He looked fifty years younger as he took the ticket.

I swear it was holy for the man.

Close to rapture, or tears, he grasped the ticket to his chest, crying out, "I have it! I have a ticket! I found the ticket!"

"You?" I said.

"Julius, I come for thee!"

Then I unleashed a grudging smile.

Scoundrel and Thief he may be, but Cousin Archibald looked *happy*—a thing I have never seen before.

When he began to dance, I admit I laughed.

He pirouetted around and out of my room. Humming. There was no pantomimed partner. Dancing with his own self was sufficient.

Selfishness runs deep.

Then came the fateful moment. Just as Archibald was about to turn towards the stairs, Tybalt, mouse hanging from his mouth, came running from the west garret. Before I could call out, before Archibald could catch hold of anything, he had tripped over the cat and tumbled headfirst down the stairs.

Upon recalling the moment, I cannot help but be impressed with the capacity of that man's lungs while tumbling through the air. His screams raised the dead, I'm sure of it.

The entire household converged on the fourth floor, Parian and Agnes out of breath, their faces red, my face white as a sheet (Agnes told me later) as we crouched around the crumpled figure. Archibald lay still, eyes wide open. Then, in an instant of recognition that something was terribly wrong, he began to rage.

He raged at me. He raged at God for creating cats. He raged at Young Hawkes (I can't understand why). He raged at staircases in general. He raged at me, again.

"Stupid, selfish curse of a woman!" he cried out. "My leg! My leg!"

I was kneeling at that point, and, upon looking at said leg, my stomach lurched. His foot was pointing in a rather unnatural direction, a complete right angle.

"Parian, run for a doctor! Agnes, go fetch Mr. Pierce. Go, now! Then boil some water and gather rags. Agnes, go!"

They went, and I was left with a pale, shaking, screaming lunatic.

It wasn't long before I heard the thunder of footsteps on the stairs and Mr. Pierce dropped down beside me.

"His left leg," I said.

All the while Archibald was screaming, "See what she did! See what she's done to me!" He kept blathering, but Mr. Pierce ignored him. He had run his hands carefully down Archibald's leg, wincing when he came to the break. "It's bad, Emma" he said, eyes focused, breathing hard, "and what I'm about to do is going to hurt like hell. Pin Mr. Flat's shoulders to the floor."

As I did so—Archibald yelling, "No, no, no!"—there came the most horrifying crunch I think I've ever heard. And Cousin Archibald, eyes bulging, lurched forward, paused, as if held at bay by an invisible force, before fainting dead on the floor.

I slouched back and looked at Mr. Pierce, who was now bent over the reset leg.

"Fetch something straight," he commanded. "And a rope or a rag."

I ran into the nearest forbidden fourth-floor bedroom and took the poker from before the fireplace. But it was too heavy, so I threw it aside. Opening a closet, I rummaged about until I found a cane.

Agnes, there with bandages when I returned, was staring at Archibald. As she began to sway, I rushed up to catch her.

"Is he dead?" she asked as she gripped my arms.

"No, he isn't. Sit down and do what Mr. Pierce says."

I handed Mr. Pierce the cane, which he took and broke over his knee. The snap was too similar to the sound of him setting the bone, and I closed my eyes a quick moment before focusing on unwinding a bandage and handing it to Mr. Pierce. He secured the cane to Archibald's leg.

"Agnes, do you have any ice in your icebox?"

"No, sir."

"Pity." Then he looked at me. "We need to get him to a bed."

"There is one just in that room there," I pointed to the empty bedroom, "but he is very attached to his own rooms on the second floor."

"If he's just below you, you'll never get any sleep. I'll carry him down while he's unconscious. Show me where to go, Miss Lion. Agnes, run and see if the doctor is coming. Bring him up to Mr. Flat's room immediately. One, two—" and on three, he'd gathered Archibald into his arms and stood. I kicked the rest of the ruined cane out of the way and led Mr. Pierce down to the second floor.

We had just laid Cousin Archibald on his bed when the voices of Parian and the doctor could be heard.

"Is he in here?" I could hear the doctor ask. Then through the door came Parian, the doctor behind him. "Let me through," said the doctor, his eyes taking in Cousin Archibald, then, in the quickest of moments, myself and Mr. Pierce. It was then he froze. "I'll be damned. If it isn't Niall Pierce!"

I was shocked.

Mr. Pierce, whose attention was still with Archibald, gave the man a second look. "What the—Fairchild? What in the blazes are you doing here?"

"The same could be asked of you. Who's the patient?"

"Mr. Archibald Flat. Snapped both his tibia and fibula. I'm afraid I acted as I would on the battlefield, resetting the bones before swelling set in."

"Good, good. How long has he been unconscious?"

"Since the resetting. Only a few minutes now."

And on they went, exchanging bits of information. Dr. Fairchild looked over the leg. "Well done. Just as I would have set it. I can bring a better splint tomorrow, but the cane is fine for now. He's going to be in a great deal of pain when he wakes." It was then that Fairchild looked around until he found me. "He will need laudanum these first days of recovery. Do you know how it is administered?"

As I was shaking my head, Mr. Pierce said, "I can help her. What's the dose?"

"Begin with twelve drops every four hours. We can adjust that if necessary. You know what you're looking for, don't you, Pierce?"

Mr. Pierce nodded. "Will you fetch the bottle now?"

"I've got some in my bag. You don't have any, do you?"

"Never touch the cursed stuff anymore, if I can help it."

I felt fairly invisible, and so I was surprised to see something else pass between them. Some unspoken history. Judging by Fairchild's expression, it was not pleasant.

Dr. Fairchild took a few more minutes examining Cousin Archibald, gave Pierce the bottle of laudanum, then asked, "What is that clenched in his hand?"

I opened Cousin Archibald's fingers and there, crushed but held fast, was the red ticket to *Julius Caesar*.

July 15th

I did not go to church this morning. All efforts, as they had all night, went towards keeping Cousin Archibald comfortable. The laudanum did its work. Except when it did not. After four hours he would wake howling. The man is in a great deal of pain.

Doctor Fairchild came first thing in the morning and rebound his leg—fortunately Cousin Archibald was asleep.

Later in the afternoon, when Archibald insisted on staying awake, I entered to sit with him. There was a fire in his room despite the warm day, and yet over his pyjamas were two silk morning robes.

"Hello, Cousin," said I, as I claimed the chair beside his bed.

Archibald's face was white, and his hands were shaking. I couldn't look at his leg without hearing the break of it in my head. I shuddered. All of me felt for his pain. The poor man.

Alas, my pity could not last long.

"Did you come to finish the job?" hissed he.

"Finish? I— No, Cousin. I am tremendously sorry for you. I came to see how—"

"You deliberately set that demon feline in my path!" panted he. (I believe he was trying to shout.) "You degenerate! You had it ALL planned from the beginning! Lure me into helping you claim a ticket, show forth an effort, then attack! Kill me off and take both tickets for yourself. Keep *Julius Caesar* for your own despotic ends! Brutus is a *saint* in comparison to you!"

"Cousin, really! I know you are in a tremendous amount of pain. We are all worried sick about you. Please, calm down!"

"I will not! You do not deserve to live!"

I vehemently disagreed with such an assessment.

"Sir! Calm yourself!"

"Never!" Archibald was quite purple in the face, and I was certain he was going to die right then and there.

He did not.

The apoplectic fit was avoided.

Unfortunate.

"Parian? Please come in!" I called out, to no avail.

Cousin Archibald was not finished. "You think you're so high and mighty. Better than all of us. Dictating every penny. Ruling this household just like the Bible said you would! Women ruling! Children running about!"

I laughed. I couldn't help it. He was sounding so ridiculous. "The Bible speaks of Lapis Lazuli? How splendid!"

"FIEND!" he shouted, the spray of his spittle on my face. "I will win! I will see you ruined! I will see you a beggar in the street before I'm through. I will see you wasted! I will see you debased! You! You, you hoyden! You Irish Bast—"

"Hold your tongue, man," came a chilling order from the door.

I turned to see Mr. Pierce, a dark expression on his face.

"She's to blame!" Archibald screamed, lifting his hands to plead with Mr. Pierce.

"Nothing of the sort," Mr. Pierce said as he walked to Archibald's bedside table and began to mix a fresh draught of laudanum. "It was a dreadful accident that Miss Lion wouldn't wish upon you."

"She would! She would! I have stolen her fortune, nearly every pound and she wishes me dead for it! I wasted it all! And now she will give *my* ticket to a less deserving soul! She's a shrew, she is!"

Beings of high quality may have let such vulgar abuse pass in understanding of the pain the man suffered. I am not one such being. After what he's done? The viper!

So I delivered my own sermon of hellfire. "You have sought every opportunity to ruin me, Archibald Flat, but your Machiavellian plans won't work! Between God and my banker, I intend to keep Lapis Lazuli House until the very day I die, and *nothing* you do will take it from me. I will come off conqueror. I will claim this victory. And you will lie quiet! Do we understand one another?"

Mr. Pierce, still occupied with the laudanum, spared the briefest glance in my direction. When I had finished, he held the glass towards the lunatic before him. "Drink," he ordered.

"Never!" And then, with a gleam that I cannot entirely blame on the feverish pallor of his face, Archibald lifted his crumpled red ticket and ate it.

I lie not.

He ate it.

He placed the ticket in his mouth, chewed, and swallowed.

Then he began to choke.

Alas, it was not to death, for Mr. Pierce handed him the waiting glass of laudanum, and Cousin Archibald took the entire dose, washing poor Caesar down his gullet.

"There," his voice cracked. "Now you cannot steal my ticket for another. A harpy like you deserves to be alone!"

My laugh was sharp. "The reason—the *only* reason—I don't throw you out on your ear is to honour the memory of my father. But beware, you bitter *coward*, for Irish ghosts keep their humour, and I will see you out of this house with his blessing if you dare cross me again. I do not relish your receiving of your just deserts, but I will not listen to you rage a moment longer. Hold your tongue and be grateful!"

Archibald was shaking, his face still deep purple, and he held his tongue for a solid ten counts before exploding with a "Bah!"

He did not, however, say anything else.

The laudanum was doing its blessed work.

Mr. Pierce's tone was even when he said, "I will sit with Mr. Flat until he is asleep again. Shall I find you afterward in the drawing room?"

I nodded and left Archibald in his capable, and somewhat terrifying, hands.

When Mr. Pierce did arrive in the drawing room, his limp in accompaniment, he looked tired. I was sitting in one corner of the green sofa, and he joined me, situating himself at the other end.

"He's asleep," Mr. Pierce said.

"Thank you. I will award you the Lapis Lazuli Cross of Honour, as soon as we have one."

It was silent for a few minutes. Then he asked, almost savagely, "Is it true?"

The force behind his words startled me, the anger palpable. He sounded like Arabella's avenging angel.

At first I thought his ire was directed towards me.

"Is what true?" I asked with a defensive edge.

"Did Mr. Flat waste your fortune?"

And the way he said *Mr. Flat* assured me it was not I, but Cousin Archibald, who was the target of his wrath.

"Did Mr. Flat *waste* your fortune?" he repeated.

I can't think of any gentleman presuming to ask such a question. But Mr. Pierce is neither a gentleman nor afraid of the difficult. As being demure is not my strength, I pulled no punches—to use a favourite term of Maxwell's.

"There was never a fortune to waste," I stated. "Well, not really. What remained of said fortune was a living. And yes, it is true; it was to be my livelihood. My banker says I've two years if a solution is not found."

"That man knowingly spent your living?" His indignation was so thoroughly righteous I could almost see a halo threatening.

He stood. Fists clenching, unclenching, clenching again as he crossed the room, and I half expected he might march upstairs and pummel Archibald in his sleep. It made me fear for my cousin's life.

Extraordinary feat that it is.

Walking from door to window and back, Mr. Pierce uttered *several* choice phrases that—seeing as it is the Sabbath—I will not record in this journal.

However marvellous they were.

It must be said that I do not need Mr. Pierce to come to my rescue—aside from what he pays by renting Lapis Lazuli Minor and the studio, *that* I need desperately—and so I said in a cavalier tone, "No need for concern, Mr. Pierce. I am managing."

"Are you indeed?" It was said in a suspect manner.

"My banker and I have a plan. Of sorts." I gave a confident chin lift. "You needn't worry on my behalf."

Mr. Pierce claimed the pink chair, lifted a hand to cover his face, and said something about horse thieves being deservedly shot.

How very American of him.

We sat a long while in silence.

And I, Emma M. Lion, the girl who once rallied an entire dormitory of boys at Stoicism, A Preparatory School for Boys to storm the kitchens and steal the mince pies set aside for their instructors, felt tired…and like I might have need of a good cry.

It has been an exhausting two weeks.

"Has Fairchild been by today?" Mr. Pierce asked, breaking the dismal silence.

"Yes. He is to come back this evening, thankfully; I do have a few questions to put to him."

Mr. Pierce frowned. "But you are to attend your play tonight?"

I lifted my hands in defeat. "I cannot leave—"

"You can. You should! Parian is here, as is Agnes. The old man will be in a drugged stupor. And I can be here when Fairchild arrives." Then an odd smile. "That wasn't your ticket he swallowed, was it?"

I couldn't help a laugh. "Indeed, no. Mine is safely upstairs in the garret."

"Go see your play, Miss Lion. Enjoy yourself. Stay late. I can help manage things here."

"I believe I shall," I answered at length.

He nodded his approval.

Then my curiosity behaved as well as his own. "Do you know Dr. Fairchild well?" I asked.

"He was a regimental doctor for a time, in Africa," came Mr. Pierce's answer. He looked about as if for something to drink and, finding nothing, stood. "I'll be over to help with Mr. Flat. Enjoy yourself tonight, Miss Lion."

"Thank you, Mr. Pierce." Then, "You seem cursed with our strange catastrophes."

Mr. Pierce looked thoughtful, rubbing the inside of his pointer finger along his chin. "Ironically, the events seem to trace back to Tybalt, the cat I introduced to Lapis Lazuli."

He was blaming himself. A ridiculous thing I could not countenance.

"It is not your fault," I replied. "A strange accident, as you said yourself."

"We cannot always predict the outcomes of our actions, Miss Lion, however well intended."

I stood. "What else is life but a string of outcomes beyond our control?"

These words sounded far more jaded than I meant them to, but Mr. Pierce was not bothered. "What else, indeed, Miss Lion?"

And he was gone.

It will be dark soon, and I am about to leave—wearing my red dress. The doctor has come, but Mr. Pierce is seeing to the visit.

I, the *hoyden* that I am, will do my best to look presentable and slip away into the night.

Later

That was the most enthusiastic performance of *Julius Caesar* I have ever seen. Brutus appeared ready to burst into song with every other word.

When I arrived at the address on the ticket, a shadow stepped out onto the walk, and instead of entering the front door of this fine Sterling Street home, I was rushed discreetly down a side garden path, lit with very few lights. I felt almost like Titania in the enchanted woods. The back doors of the house were flung open, and the loveliest array of fabrics were draped about, illuminated by candlelight, all leading to a ballroom with a curtained stage at one end.

I was shown to my seat by a young man wearing a mask of the prime minister's face; and, lo and behold, who was already seated beside it, glancing over a programme, looking as ordered as a pocket watch?

Islington, The Duke of.

As I claimed my seat, he took note, his hazel eyes appraising my red gown.

"How very Roman of you, Miss Lion."

"Hello, Islington."

"Would you like to look at my programme?" he offered, the appropriate amount of boredom and condescension dressing his tone.

"Why thank you."

I glanced over the programme and made a dissatisfied noise. It had been a taxing day. A taxing week. And whereas I usually enjoy St. Crispian's quirks, tonight I found myself slightly put off by them.

"The programme does not list the names of the players," I said lightly, handing it back to Islington.

"No. *To be revealed*," he quoted, the words written by each character's name.

"Then what is the point of the programme?" I asked, *pointedly*.

The duke shrugged. "What is the point of the entire production, Miss Lion? To be amused. This"—he held up the programme—"is amusing."

I did not find it so. Which was a failing on my part. Usually, it would have been the sort of thing I would be pleased to keep. Archibald had certainly stained the whole affair.

The room continued to fill with those lucky enough to have secured tickets, the room abuzz with whispers and half-laughs. I tapped my fingers against my reticule.

"I note that you are alone," Islington said.

"I am. My elderly cousin, who was to accompany me this evening, has met with disaster and is in bed with a broken leg."

"Horrible for him, I am sure. My apologies." Then, "Did you have no one else to give the ticket? That scoundrel named Jack, for example?"

The look I sent him was not benign. "The extra ticket also met with an unfortunate accident."

"You astonish me," Islington answered, sounding anything but astonished. "Dare I ask?"

"My cousin ate it."

Now the duke's seal of self-approval was broken, and he looked at me with an unbelieving amusement. "You're joking."

"I only wish I were."

"Was it an accident?"

"Oh, no. Spite to be sure. He claimed to have put in such hard work to earn a ticket, he wasn't going to give it away to a less deserving soul. His words, not mine."

"Remarkable."

It was then the lights dimmed and the curtain began to rustle.

"I didn't see you scampering about St. Crispian's after any clues," I whispered.

Islington looked at me—it was a glance, really—then gave his attention back to the curtain. "And yet here I am."

"By the grace of God goes Islington," I murmured as the curtains opened.

"Indeed, Miss Lion," he answered in return.

It was vastly entertaining. The players were brilliant, the aforementioned Brutus a bit too bright in his role as he declared, "Judge me, you gods!" There was a good deal of laughter when some of the scenery tumbled onto the floor of the Senate, but all in all, a very good production.

At intermission we were all treated to a dessert and a cup of tea. Islington only accepted the tea.

"You're not going to have dessert?" I asked, and justly so. It looked positively mouthwatering.

"No," Islington answered. "I don't care for cherry and chocolate together."

"Now, if you had written that in your diary of five years ago, I would know," I replied.

His sideways glance was unsettling. "Wisdom would make as little reference to that whole affair as possible, Miss Lion."

"I'm sure you're right," I sighed. "When a man has a Rabbit Room, one must tread lightly or—"

"Or what?"

I took a sip of tea, then looked at him rather directly. "Or he may '*Cry Havoc! and let slip the dogs of war.*'"

Islington couldn't help but laugh. He looked very dapper doing so, his hair combed back, his hazel eyes alight, his collar so white it was blinding. Then, closing his eyes in a moment of reverie, he repeated the full line, "'*Ranging for revenge, with Até by his side come hot from hell, shall in these confines with a Monarch's voice cry 'Havoc!' and let slip the dogs of war.*'"

I smiled. "You are wasted as a duke. You ought to have been a Marc Antony."

"'*Friends, Romans, countrymen, lend me your ears*,'" he quoted dryly.

"Just so."

"Would you have done it?" the duke then asked.

"Spoken at Caesar's burial?"

"Killed him in the first place."

Of all the questions I have ever been asked in my life, this must be the strangest.

"I don't rightly know," I answered. "I've never read Plutarch's *Lives.* Faulty education, if you remember. Would you have?"

He seemed to be taking the question seriously. "In some ways, I feel for Brutus. I've always been moved, reasonably or unreasonably, when he states, '*not that I loved Caesar less, but that I loved Rome more.*'"

"Because of your obligations to queen and country, and the stern legacy of your father?"

We both froze. The words spilled out before I'd thought them through, spoken as if he'd shared his private concerns willingly, rather than my having read them without sanction.

I was appalled with myself. And blame my complete error in judgement on the exhaustion of the day and the intoxicating setting in which we found ourselves.

But Islington, who I had expected to cut me rather severely with his sharp tongue—a lashing I *fully* deserved—took a thoughtful breath and, without looking at me, said, "God as my witness, Miss Lion, serving Rome carries a price that at times— Well, never mind that."

And before I could think of anything to say, the lights dimmed, the curtains went up, and onto Act Four we marched.

Upon returning home, I opened the door and was met by the drawing room light spilling into the hall. Taking off my hat, and setting my gloves and programme—Islington having handed it to me as he left—on the sideboard, I entered the drawing room not a little surprised to find The Tenant stretched out on the green sofa, his head against a cushion, ankles crossed, shirtsleeves rolled up; he was reading a newspaper. There was, I noted, a glass of something on the floor beside him. For his sake, I hoped it was strong.

"Mr. Pierce! Good evening."

Glancing up at me, he swung his feet down and set himself aright, placing the paper next to him as he stood. He looked apologetic.

"I'm, uh. Pardon. Only, I've been helping Parian. He requested I remain until you returned home. To use his exact words, I was not to leave him 'to the cruel vicissitudes of caring for the ill.'"

"Of course. No need to explain. Do sit down, please." I motioned as I sat on the chair across from him.

Once settled, he said, "How is Caesar? Dead, I presume?"

"Very much so. A small miracle as Brutus looked more inclined to give us a musical revue than a tragedy with himself as villain."

Mr. Pierce's laugh was low. "Villain or hero?"

"The endless debate," I rejoined. "How is Mr. Flat? *Not* dead, I presume?"

He shook his head. "Very much alive, despite being steeped in laudanum. Fairchild confirmed my suspicions. Mr. Flat's recovery is going to be difficult. Walking without a cane, most likely impossible. Walking with a cane? Hopeful, but one never knows. This will change Mr. Flat's ability to go about. And before he can even try to walk, he will be bedridden for some time."

It was, I admit, a gloomy prediction. I uttered, "Oh dear. Poor man. And we are all in for it."

"Aye, there's the rub," he quoted dryly. "I can't imagine it easy for you to deal with the man when all is well and good, to say nothing of his current state."

"Not very easy, no."

"He was yelling at you something fierce earlier today." He paused then, and I believe—as they say in novels—his eyes hardened, or sharpened, or something. "Does he treat you that way often? After what he's done to you?"

At which point, I was at a loss. One cannot explain Cousin Archibald's behaviour without appearing an absolute lunatic for putting up with it.

Oh dear.

Am I a lunatic?

Well.

Damned by my own tongue. Or pen, rather.

Mr. Pierce insisted on waiting for an answer, so I said, "He is not always so vocal." (That is not necessarily true.) "Yet I admit he is his own brand of terror. We all have a cross to carry, Mr. Pierce," I added philosophically. "Mine is this somewhat grotesque old man who, as you heard, considers me a hoyden."

He smiled, but it was token. His eyes rather too serious.

"I find his actions despicable," he said.

"As do I."

"Why do you allow him to stay?"

There it was. The haunted hound of a question.

I began with what I've told everyone else. "My father wished me to be kind, and—"

"That isn't it," he interrupted. A bit bold of him, I thought. And then, "No father would wish this on his daughter. You have been severely misused. Mr. Flat should be prosecuted."

"No grounds. The law—"

"The law be hanged."

"There are no grounds," I repeated.

"So what is it? The real reason? I don't believe it's your father."

This is the conversation I have been having privately with myself the last three months. And my father's request, a very real consideration, has always stood shadow over the other reason, the underneath reason. Pressing my lips together, looking at the floor, I took a stab at what felt an impossible explanation.

I told Mr. Pierce how we lived in a cottage, my parents and I. There was a wood with a river. A garden. A hill for walking. Laughter in the kitchen where my mother arranged flowers and my father painted. It was, in a word, the only word. Home.

I braved a look at him. "They both died within the same year, and home was taken. Gone. I've not been back since. Couldn't bear it, I think, to see others living in our places. It was such a wrench. To be ripped away. To scramble for earth and air. To find some of that sense in a person only to lose it again. I— I can't bear it, Mr. Pierce. Can't bear to think of it. The pain of losing home. And so, knowing the acute sense of loss, how can I take this man's home? However horrible he may be. However undeserving of mercy. Do you understand?"

Mr. Pierce looked sad, in a way. "I do. I know of what you speak."

"I've been asking myself that very same question. That, I think, is why."

He gave a single nod. "All right then."

Uncomfortable, I stood. Mr. Pierce followed suit, picking up his newspaper.

"It's messier than we ever imagined it to be as children," he said.

"What?"

"Life." And that expression of his that I had seen over tea—the one where he felt guilty for something. For the imposition of his presence? For still being alive?—flooded his face. He cleared his throat. "I'll be working in the salon, Miss Lion. Call me for anything you need. And tell Mr. Flat that if he gives you an ounce of trouble—"

"You'll defend my honour?"

My quirked smile was meant as a humorous end to the night, but Mr. Pierce blinked. "I would never presume—"

"I am teasing, Mr. Pierce. And I—I do thank you for having done just that. It was comforting, strange as that sounds. I'm always managing him on my own—well, since my parents died. To have another guarding my back is a missed familiarity." I was looking, not just feeling, flustered, and I finished badly with, "Your helping me felt like…home."

"That elusive shore," he said quietly.

“Aye.”

“Goodnight then, Miss Lion.”

“Goodnight.”

And I hadn’t realised until that moment how much I’ve missed that feeling, of someone inside your four walls watching out for you. The feeling that home isn’t just a place, but also people. I’ve forgotten it could be.

Now I’m growing maudlin.

Time to blow out the candle.

July 18th

The entire house is upside down.

Agnes is burning the food.

Parian is disappearing and, might I speculate, inebriated?

Cousin Archibald is a misery.

And the task has been left to me to deliver the man his laudanum.

I'm trying not to rely on Mr. Pierce. He spends his days in his studio, the place strewn with boxes and photographs and who knows what else.

I have also almost sworn off the entire institution of writing in one's journal. My hand is cramped, I've stayed up late into the night writing an unseemly amount, and I am blue-devilled as a result.

Now I am going to go wash the ink stains off my fingers.

There is no good humour to be had at Lapis Lazuli House.

July 19th

I was just out in the back garden when Agnes came to find me.

"Miss Lion. Are you at home to visitors?"

I laughed. "Am I at home to visitors?"

"My mother's last letter said fine ladies expect their maids to say that."

"Ah. Well. To whom am I at home?"

"He said his name is Hawkes? He's the one who helped when you came home—"

"Young Hawkes? The vicar?"

Agnes bunched her freckled nose. "He doesn't look like a vicar."

No, Agnes, he certainly does not.

"Will you take him some tea? I'll be in soon."

To the garret went I, making myself look ~~very~~ mildly presentable, and then down to the drawing room.

Hawkes was not sitting. Instead, he was standing at the window, looking out at the street, hands behind his back, a furrow in his brow. His hair was mildly askew.

"Young Hawkes."

He looked at me, rocking back on his feet. "Miss Lion."

I could see that Agnes had left him with tea, but Hawkes hadn't touched it.

"Is the tea not to your liking?"

"It is, thank you. I am only waiting for it to cool."

We sat.

"It's an unexpected pleasure to see you at Lapis Lazuli House, Young Hawkes. Have you come to ensure I've not fallen into more degenerate habits since our last encounter?"

He gave the flicker of a smile. "Thank you, no. I've come about Mr. Flat."

I slouched somewhat in my chair. "Yes."

"Fairchild said it was quite a break."

This caught my attention. "You spoke with the doctor?"

"I did."

"But how did you know he was the attending physician?"

Hawkes took a sip of his tea. "Fairchild is often required at Traitors Road. Young men doing foolish things. When I heard what had happened to Mr. Flat, I suspected Fairchild might have been at hand."

So Young Hawkes knows Dr. Fairchild, and Dr. Fairchild knows Mr. Pierce. Does that mean that Young Hawkes knows Mr. Pierce? I have yet to see my Tenant at church, and he seems to be...what would be the word...*sceptical* of religion?

"Is he in a good deal of pain?" Hawkes asked.

"When the laudanum wears off, yes."

"I thought I would sit with him for a while, if you don't mind."

Mind? No, I did not mind.

I took him up to the second floor, where a groggy Archibald Flat was laying prostrate on his bed, being attended to by Parian Under Duress.

"Parian, Young Hawkes is here to sit with Mr. Flat."

"Thank the good Lord," Parian said before fleeing the room.

I watched from the doorway as Young Hawkes took the chair, moved it to the window, sat, pulled a book from his pocket, opened it up, and then ignored the book while he looked with concerned eyes towards the slumbering demon in the bed.

It looked, for a moment, as if he cared.

July 23rd

My life—the simple life I see when I close my eyes, where I am a student of the classics, of science, of history, keeping my appointments with plenty of time to expand the perimeters of my mind—seems to be getting away from me.

Occasionally when walking in the park, I come across a desperate soul attempting to keep pace with a large, insistent hound. They end up being yanked about, tripping over their own shoes. This is how I feel just now. July has been its own whirlwind—fairly occupied with Caesar, granted, but I have hardly read a thing.

This was not what I envisioned in March. How green I was. How young! How inexperienced!

I now know better.

If I do not carve out my own time to study, the extent of my education will be a dismal combination of Aunt Eugenia's lectures, Cousin Archibald's screams, and Young Hawkes's sermons.

The latter being acceptable, especially when containing poetry.

I ought to give up my illusion of ownership and simply borrow books from Aunt Eugenia's library.

A thought which depresses.

I so love to scribble on the pages.

A fresh conversation atop one long since written.

Later

I lit a candle for Father tonight.

July 24th

I've just returned from a few errands—new thread, buttons, butcher's string for Agnes—which culminated in a small tea at Everett's. The intention was Tea for One, the One being myself. But the Fates, humorous when delving out my portion of existence, had another thing in mind. For not two minutes had passed before a shadow slipped into the seat across from me and became flesh. I glanced up and grimaced.

"Oh, Jack," I sighed. "I forgot you plagued this city."

The crocodile grinned. "Hello, wife of my youth."

"How very proverbial of you," I replied. "Have you been reading your Bible?"

"No time for reading, Miss Lion. The pace of the world is changing, and we must change with it."

"Yes, well, off with you then. Go keep the pace."

A smirk in response, and Jack lifted his hand to signal the serving girl bring another cup to the table.

It was then that I decided to put Jack to good use.

"If you are joining me, Mr. Hollingstell, perhaps you ought to pay the bill. It would be most gallant."

He looked over at the single scone on my plate, then at the vast loneliness of the otherwise empty table. "Your little cat lap looks like it needs a sponsor."

"Cat lap?"

"Oh, don't tell me the estimable Miss Lion doesn't know her thieves' Latin?"

"Pardon?"

"Jargon, Miss Lion. Slang."

Before I could say anything, the serving girl returned with a cup and saucer for Jack. After a few enquiries into the menu, he ordered a much fuller tea than I had, and, shaking out his napkin and placing it over his lap, as pleased as a mouse in a cheese shop.

Though Jack Hollingstell is no mouse.

It was not too long before a three-tiered wonder appeared at our table. He considered the mountain of baked goods with self-satisfaction.

"Heavens, Jack. For a man as trim as you are, you certainly adore pastries."

"I find myself running about a good deal," he remarked glibly.

"From the authorities, I presume?"

Eyeing me with humour, he accepted the tea I prepared for him.

I helped myself to a puff pastry with pink and white icing. "Have you come to exact one of your favours? You only have two, I remind you."

He smiled. "No. I intend to keep those safe until absolutely necessary."

"Then why are you here?"

"Because, *crème de la crème*, I want to ask you a question."

"Oh? What do I get for answering?"

"A decent tea, unless you prefer I slip out, leaving you to foot the bill, sweets."

Ah. He had me pinned.

"What do you wish to know?"

Jack finished an entire eclair before responding with the satisfaction of a snake after consuming a rodent—I lie not, he sighed with contentment. "I love one thing in this world, Miss Lion."

"Yourself?"

Jack grinned. "I love *two* things in this world, Miss Lion. Myself"—he made a grand gesture of self-appreciation—"and sweet pastries. Now, to my question. How much do you know of Mary's professor?"

"Mary's professor?"

"Yes. The man who has her spending most evenings typing his notes about the East India Company instead of traipsing about London with me."

I knew nothing, but I sipped my tea as if I knew everything. "Why?"

"I have my reasons."

Which wasn't enough incentive to divulge any information.

"Very well." That was it. I was expecting to be pressed or cajoled or anything, but Jack said nothing more. We finished our tea, Jack paid the bill, and then, as I was pulling on my gloves, he disappeared. Out the door before I could blink.

It is impressive. And maddening.

As I was about to leave, the serving girl rushed up to me with a small box. "This is for you, Miss."

"Oh, I didn't order anything else." And I certainly wasn't going to pay for it.

She flushed pink. "It is a gift from the gentleman."

I refrained from pointing out that Jack is no gentleman. "Is it?"

"Yes." Then her flush turned towards a very uncomfortable red. "I am to tell you it's to help you keep a sweet tongue in your head."

I laughed. And it took me a good thirty seconds to stop. Relieved I'd not taken offence, the serving girl handed me the box and I thanked her.

Now, sitting at my desk—having dropped the coins I would have spent into a jar for the bank—I've opened my box and found six apple tartlets, snug and happy, ready to meet their demise.

Agnes will share in the spoils because she is good.

Parian will share in the spoils because he is being constantly berated by Cousin Archibald.

As for the cantankerous, old crow? Well. Perhaps one. For pity.

July 25th

Mary,

I've had a visit from your slippery eel of a false cousin. He wanted to know what I knew of your professor, whose notes you type in the evenings? Two questions: Why is Jack wondering? And is there something amiss with said professor?

I've not seen you in over a fortnight. Let us remedy this.

Emma

Emma the worried,

There is nothing to concern yourself over. Jack, as ever, likes mischief and information. I'm leaving London for a week, to watch my brother's children while he and his wife go to the seaside, an ideal place to take children, in my estimation. My brother, however, is not a very nice man, as we both know.
Do not worry over Jack.

Mary

Mary who plays with fire,

Telling someone not to worry over Jack is like letting loose a tiger and inviting it for tea. In my case, quite literally.

Have a jolly time with your nieces and nephews. Teach them to whistle "Come into the Garden, Maud" on repeat, and see if it doesn't drive your brother mad.

We will speak more on this subject when you return.
Be warned.

Emma

July 26th

Arabella invited me for tea today.

I knew why and almost cried off.

Had I not just enjoyed a luxurious cat lap?

Arabella ordered an expansive and expensive tea—"Let us fatten ourselves up, Emma. We do deserve it."—and while we were waiting for it to arrive, Arabella did something I've rarely seen her do. She allowed enough worry to show on her face as to cause three wrinkles, one between her eyebrows and two along her brow.

I quietly braced myself.

"Will you be well tomorrow?"

I did not want to be flippant, Arabella having offered her peerless face to the cause, but I had very little to say to anyone on the subject.

"I expect I shall be fine."

"Hmm."

Tea arrived, and, the wrinkle having vanished, we began to work away at the mound set before us. If I were tempting fate, I would set Arabella and Jack up for a tea. They would do it so well.

"I wasn't with you last year, you know," Arabella said after a while. "Or the year before that."

Thankfully, I didn't have to answer as my mouth was too full.

She looked at me rather directly. "You don't have to be alone this year."

I swallowed. "I shall be fine, Arabella. I want only a nice walk, a long afternoon of reading, and perhaps a bath. Seeing as how your mother has given me no orders, I expect a quiet, lovely day at my leisure."

Arabella surprised me again by looking thoughtful. "I am not convinced a quiet day is what you need."

"What on earth do you suggest? Shall we storm Parliament instead?"

Arabella smiled. "My trouble never goes in a political direction, Emma."

"Well, my trouble doesn't discriminate."
"It certainly does not," Arabella smirked.
She took a sip of tea, and the unpleasant subject was dropped.
Tomorrow will be as any other day.
I'm almost sure of it.

July 27th

When I woke this morning, my eyes still closed, tangled in the bedclothes after too warm a night, I knew something was terribly wrong, yet I could not remember what. It was as if I walked a dreamscape, with no power to change or understand what oppressed me.

Then, upon opening my eyes, I remembered.

I shut them again and rolled over, burying myself under my blanket.

It is the twenty-seventh of July.

Agnes eventually knocked on my door.

"Are you in there, Miss? Are you well?"

Biting my bottom lip hard enough to cause pain—unintentionally drawing blood—I forced myself to sit up. "Yes, Agnes. I took the luxury of a slow morning."

"Shall I bring breakfast up to you now? Or something for midday?"

I almost said yes, but I know my limits and could easily have spent the entire day in bed.

"No, I will come down to the dining room."

"Why not the breakfast room? It has such nice windows."

At this point I swung my legs over the side of the bed and thought that Agnes was overworked.

"We do not have a breakfast room, Agnes."

"Of course we do! It's— Oh no. Pardon, Miss Lion. I forgot Mr. Flat said the room carried bad memories and you never, ever, ever were to be reminded of it. Pity. It's such a nice little room. Something truly horrible must have happened to make you fear it so."

"What are you talking about, Agnes? Where is this room?"

"Behind the drawing room, the second door off the hallway."

"That's a room for storage."

"'Tisn't. It's a breakfast room with two lovely windows."

I paused long enough for a weary breath.

"Does Archibald use it?"

"Oh no. Doesn't care for it, he says. No one's used it all the while I've been at Lapis Lazuli House, but I've kept it clean."

In that moment I hated him. I truly *hated* him. My stoic, charitable, eroding response to all his treachery was unravelling for this small, stupid thing.

"I will take my breakfast in the breakfast room, Agnes, just to spite the old addlepate."

I fetched my worn dress, the grey one, too tired to be anything but comfortable, and, though the clock was leaning towards noon, I pulled my hair back in a messy braid rather than pinning it into a style more suitable for my age. Washing my face, I picked up my journal from my desk and came downstairs.

As I passed the second floor hallway, I glared towards Archibald's closed door.

I may have even sent a hex.

One cannot be sure.

True to her word, Agnes led me past the drawing room to a door with a lock, one that I had always been told was storage—one my father had always been told was storage—Agnes prattling on about having the key. When she unlocked the door and pushed it open, I blinked, and very nearly cried.

It was lovely. It *is* lovely. I am sitting in it now, feeling as if I'm in a different world altogether. A leaf-green paint on the walls, cream trim around the two narrow windows, a set of built-in shelves filled entirely with unused flower vases from a century past. There is a painting of a coast—Irish? And another of a little boy who I suspect might be my father. Ah, there. I think I see something on the top shelf.

A book. It's an illustrated book of flowers. How charming.

Agnes just brought my meal—a full breakfast *and* a full midday spread—and said, "Oh Miss Lion, you look so sad!"

"No, Agnes. I am only tired."

Neither of us are convinced.

Later

It is early evening now. I am up in my garret.

The day has gone in an…unexpected way.

Before I'd left the breakfast room, Agnes came to find me. She told me that Mr. Pierce had knocked on the salon door. "He asked if you were home, Miss. I told him I didn't know."

Sitting back in my chair, I replied, "Whyever did you tell him that, Agnes? You know very well I'm right here."

She shook her head and, with a wide-eyed expression, said, "He's so…and you're, well…it's only…so I thought…ooch. Ya ken?"

No, I did not *ken*, Agnes.

Leaving a half-eaten breakfast and Agnes's Scottish moment behind, I walked through the hall to the salon door. I lifted my hand three times—practicing the smile I would give—before I had the courage to knock. After I did, there came heavy footfalls towards me. The door swung open—goodness, that man can swing a door almost as well as he can throw open a curtain.

"Hello," I said. "You were looking for me?"

I felt rather ~~exposed~~ unmoored in that moment, nothing to hold onto.

Mr. Pierce did not make it any easier. Giving no verbal response, he considered my face; the bags under my eyes, the tired tilt of my lips, the wild attempt to braid my hair. Belligerence is not far behind sorrow for Emma M. Lion, and so I raised an eyebrow and studied him back.

The Tenant always has a degree of the haunt about him, his eyes more mirage than stone. Staring at me as if he were a spectre, he said, "It's the twenty-seventh of July."

His voice, the jaded angle of it, made his statement more flesh and blood than he.

"It is."

"How are you holding up?"

My answer was the lack of one.

"Come in." He stepped back, opening the door wide enough to let me pass.

I did.

When I entered, the room was still in flux, things here and there, boxes scattered, odds and ends in piles. I didn't mind.

It looked how I felt.

Or rather feel, present tense.

More than I admit.

"I'm sorting, deciding what goes where," he said, prompted only by my mute study. "Go ahead, have a seat." He motioned towards the sofa, and so I walked through the small maze and sat.

"I like how the blue paint is settling," I told him.

He glanced up towards me while his hands continued to sort. "As do I."

When I said nothing in return, he looked back at his papers and stated, "The Battle of Maiwand. Three years ago today. Nine hundred and sixty-nine British and Indian soldiers dead, to say nothing of the casualties sustained by the Pashtun warriors."

I answered nothing. I had nothing *to* answer.

He worked in silence as I settled in the corner, sitting at a diagonal so that I could see Mr. Pierce from the corner of my eye while watching the street.

"Tell me about him, your friend," Mr. Pierce said at length. He was not looking at my face, which I was thankful for, allowing me privacy with his request.

Excepting Mary, it was the first time that someone who had not ever known Maxwell had asked me about him.

Unexpected. And somehow it felt like someone slipping a key through prison bars.

So, after sitting quiet a quarter of an hour, I spoke of Maxwell. Of the first time I recall him traipsing across my young girl memory. Of the summer days beyond the river. Of the secret notes between children. Of realising it was more. Of choosing one another, somehow, before we understood what it meant.

Of his leaving.

Of his death.

Hours passed, slowly, halting as often as my words did. All the while, Mr. Pierce worked steadily, his brow furrowed, his mind seemingly elsewhere. But when I said anything clever or mischievous, a smile whispered across his face. The proof of his attention.

When I described the day, the awful, heat-ridden, parched day I found out Maxwell was dead, Mr. Pierce stopped his work and watched my profile, as I was speaking more towards the window than him. He listened, and I spoke of it more completely than I've ever allowed myself to even think of it. The day, the wait, the memorial without a body.

What Evelyn said and did I kept to myself. Not even Arabella knows that.

At some point, I'd pulled my feet up beneath my skirts, curled up in the corner of the sofa, and closed my eyes.

Feeling foolish.

Feeling brave.

Having ripped something open, confiding in a man who, while not a complete stranger, is still an unknown country. Perhaps that's why I could do such a thing.

And then what I thought was only a moment later, a voice called me awake from across the room, Mr. Pierce telling me it was evening. I'd slept for hours.

I stood and faced the windows—the day outside growing dark—and wiped my hands beneath my eyes, attempting some measure of decorum. Then I thanked Mr. Pierce—rather badly—and made my way towards the door.

"Miss Lion?"

Emma M. Lion is no coward, I am pleased to report, for I turned to face him.

He did not look comfortable when he said, "We do not know one another very well, and so what I'm about to say may be erroneous."

I meant to laugh but made a strange sound instead, reminiscent of a dying animal. "You say that after today?" I quipped.

He smiled sadly. "You have a humour about you, a good deal of natural pluck, for lack of a better word. A general devil-may-care approach to some very serious circumstances."

I couldn't tell in the moment, and can't decipher now, if he meant his words to be a compliment or a subtle admonition.

"I make a go of it, when I can. It's not my disposition to…what I mean to say is, I learned a long time ago that my happiness has to be separate from the things beyond my control."

"Admirable," he said, as if he didn't believe me.

"Necessary," I answered, feeling the need to defend myself.

"Most of us understand that in theory, but we don't do it half so well as you seem to."

"It isn't my nature to choose sadness if I can help it," I said, shrugging to excuse my failure today. "Gloomy days stand in their place, but there is too much,"—I waved a hand about—"too much of everything else, I suppose, to live under them."

"And yet you carry about your ghost," he said. "You look for him over your shoulder."

I took my breath in quickly. His words hurt in the way that truth does when you wish it was a lie but know you cannot claim it to be.

"It's not a criticism," Mr. Pierce continued.

"Then what is it?" I replied, stiffly.

"It's a hope—that you don't have to carry the dead for very long."

If any other had spoken those words, I would have… Well, I'm not certain what I would have done. But the map I had drawn him of Maxwell, the confessions of the afternoon—mine in word, his in silence—allowed for him to say such a thing.

"I carry more ghosts than you could imagine, Miss Lion. I know the weight. It is no life."

I was slow to answer the honesty of his confession, but when I did, I made the fool's promise of, "I will be myself tomorrow."

And I left.

Now I'm pacing my garret.

My windows are open, and someone on Whereabouts Lane is playing a melancholy tin whistle.

Too tired to go out, too awake to stay put, I'm feeling torn, a piece of paper ripped through.

One ought not speak so freely of difficult things. Confide such grievances. No. Not freely. I did not speak freely. Every word demanded a price. Perhaps it was not too high a price to pay for understanding, but certainly too high to ever do it again.

But why not have told one who knows the toll demanded by war?

My indomitable if not grotesque humour can almost feel the restless spirit of Aunt Eugenia climbing in the garret window to tell me off.

There now. I've made myself laugh for the first time today.

July 28th

Dear Evelyn,

I was happy to receive your letter in May. You sounded like your old self, which allows me hope you are doing well. I know the date on this letter is too close to the anniversary of Maxwell's death, but I suppose that is why I write, to ask if your parents are still considering bringing him home to be buried at Barrows Edge?

Tell me, please, so that I might be present at the service. It would mean a great deal, I think. To be a part of seeing him home.

I am well in most respects, and find humour in what is left. My Cousin Archibald is still, what was it you called him? Half the world's foolish vanity poured into one soul? He is just that. Only worse, if you can imagine.

We both know your father would have little interest in my regards, but would you give them to your mother? I am very fond of her.

I dreamt of Maxwell last night. It was a disjointed affair, half at Spencer Court, half here in London, with all the wrong people in the wrong places. Nothing fit, except near the end when I saw Maxwell crossing the bridge in the back pasture of Spencer Court. You were there, coming up the hill with Damian and Arabella. I was a few steps beyond you, but Maxwell was still ahead of us all. You were saying something about refusing to fish at all costs, which sounds like you. It was comfortable as a well-worn memory, but felt very far away. A golden age passed…

Please write.

Emma

July 29th

A dinner with Aunt Eugenia.

An intimate party of twelve. Six gentlemen, five ladies, and myself.

Aunt praised me for portraying a poor, somewhat downcast soul with aplomb.

"How Arabella shined this evening! And your tragic sighs really did the trick, leaving you undesirable and tedious. The eligible suitors took note and enjoyed Arabella's smiles all the more. I'm proud of you, Emma. Here, have five pounds."

July 30th

This afternoon is not fit for man, nor beast, nor Emma M. Lion in the garret.

I kept the windows wide open all night, but still no relief.

Now there are flies in the house.

July 31st

The doctor has taken Cousin Archibald off the full dose of laudanum.

What only felt like a symbolic hell—due to the heat—is now very much a reality at Lapis Lazuli House. My own mood no exception.

I bid adieu to July.

> *IT'S BLOODY HOT.*
>
> *It is, Mr. Pierce. It is.*
>
> *HAVE YOU SEEN TYBALT ABOUT? HE'S NOT COME FOR HIS DINNER.*
>
> *He's languishing in the west garret, while the mice run a gentleman's club not three feet away.*
>
> *LAZY ~~BAST~~ SCOUNDREL.*
>
> *Indeed. To both your intended and your amended sentiment.*

August 1st

Life never fails you in this one thing: There is always an unexpected sleight of hand.

Mary showed her face at Lapis Lazuli this morning.

"Happy August to you, Emma," she said when I came downstairs.

"And good riddance to July," was my response, with a hint of vehemence.

"Was *Julius Caesar* so bad?"

"Not at all. But the circumstances surrounding it have been trying."

Mary suggested we discuss it while walking about the park. Which was golden, for in that very moment, Cousin Archibald began screaming from his bed chamber.

"Why don't we discuss the difficulties of your life, Mary. Mine have the tendency to bite."

We decided to be bold and show our faces at Hyde Park, however high the chances were of seeing too many of the Respectable sort (my most ~~esteemed~~ dictatorial aunt among them).

Beginning our leisurely rounds, I asked Mary how her brother was.

"Dreadful as always, but I like his wife," she answered, with her usual frankness. "As they were away for most of the visit, I had the run of the place, with only the children and dogs to keep alive."

"Well done, you."

Mary grinned. "And not a single broken bone to boot. I know this for fact because my brother forced the children out of bed and examined them all before saying, 'I can see you at least kept them alive.' To which my sister-in-law braved, 'And now grumpy, dear, for you have woken them all.'"

"Good for Mable," I grinned.

Mable had been a mouse of a girl upon her marriage to Mary's brother. Or so says Mary. Recently, however, she has been acquiring a voice. It does not sit well with her husband.

"And how did he take this latest push of independent thought?" I questioned.

"He's had the misfortune of falling in love with Mable. Which makes it difficult."

Well!

After discussing further demerits of Mary's brother, I claimed the promised conversation: Jack's peculiar interest in Mary's professor.

"Why, Mary?" I asked, shooting my question like a gun.

Mary sidestepped the bullet and answered sunnily, "Why does Jack have interest in anything, Emma? His own entertainment. The professor I work for is harmless. He's a widower with three children—all boys—who spends his days lecturing at university and his nights writing his book. Which is where I come in, as you know, typing notes and making revisions. I now know more about the East India Company than I ever wanted to."

Considering Mary occasionally drops one or two of these facts over tea, I gave a silent *Amen*. "You see?" Mary continued. "Perfectly harmless."

"You call a widower with three children harmless?" I retorted.

Mary looked at me blankly. Then the scales fell away and she began to laugh. "Oh dear. Never. *Never!* He's harmless." It must be recorded that Mary hesitated before adding, "Believe me, Emma."

The day Emma M. Lion believes a widower with three children to be harmless is the day she'll cast herself into the Thames.

"So, you've met this professor?"

"Not exactly. We have a mutual acquaintance who arranged the work."

"Ah. Sight unseen. Then you don't really know if he's nefarious or not."

"Emma," Mary was swinging her parasol like a sword, "if one could tell a nefarious character simply by looking at him, it would be a very different world."

I laughed. And informed her to take care, lest her professor was hunting for a strapping young wife to take up the job. "Imagine you, a stepmother!" A thought which caused us both to fall about in such a fit of laughter that we did not recover until coming face to face with Lady Stanton, who only approves fits of temper.

August 2nd

Parian, it seems, has hit a crisis point. He claims he's lost his mind. I very much doubt that, although there is no question he may have misplaced it. For Cousin Archibald is determined to make us suffer.

Having never particularly seen eye to eye on anything, Parian and I have found ourselves grudgingly on the same side of a brutal war. I would not say we've created a bond. Oh, no. Only a desperate understanding of how horrible Archibald is ~~when injured~~.

"It isn't that Mr. Flat never before shouted, Miss," Agnes said this morning. "It's that he used to spend a portion of his time shouting at other people. Now that he never leaves the house, we get the full dose, and I can't hear anything else in my head!"

I fully agreed with this assessment and answered in a dull voice, "At least London is spared."

Luckily, his shouting can only carry on for so long before he falls asleep. It is then the duty of the entire household to carry on as quietly as possible. I, for example, do not put my shoes on until I am at the front door.

Tragedy forces us all to make sacrifices.

Later

A day of great triumph!

I am in possession of a new book.

It is very short, an essay, in actuality—but I live in a somewhat delusional hope it will feel bookish on my shelf.

The essay was acquired while I paid Mr. Pierce a visit in his studio, still in the throes of disorganization. We spoke of featherweight subjects of no importance while he maneuvered about. I myself was sitting on the sofa. It was comfortable. Solid ground, despite the unmentionable events of July the 27th.

During our conversation, I declared my goal to better educate myself. I believe I said something like, "I must march forward before my desire has flown and I become one of those contented souls chained to their small routine, all the while *believing* themselves to be free. Don't think I mind a routine, that's just what I'm craving. But the right routine. My routine. Two walks a day, several hours of reading, perhaps one visit with someone I enjoy. One dinner or entertainment per week if you must, possibly two, but please let there be reading."

Mr. Pierce offered an amused expression as he sorted, making the verb a very masculine and, I admit, attractive thing. "You have a wild idealism, Miss Lion."

"Is it so unreasonable to expect a small amount of perfection from life?"

Just then Archibald could be heard hollering at Parian.

Mr. Pierce raised his eyebrows in answer, then asked, "What are you reading?"

"Nothing at present," I admitted. And explained that my own personal library was obliterated because of rather exceptional circumstances. "A story for another day," I added when he looked moderately interested. (At least I flatter myself he looked moderately interested, preferable to imagining he is moderately disinterested in what I have to say.) "I own the Bible, *The Complete Works of Shakespeare*, and *Shakespeare's Comedies, In Full*, and *Jane Eyre*, which I've read at least seven times."

And as I am committed to the truth, I must record what he uttered next, however blasphemous.

"Too much Shakespeare."

That is what he said. Those three words formed in such an ugly way.

What could the man possibly have been thinking?

"Is there such a thing!" I defended.

Mr. Piece looked up then. "When it composes a full fifty percent of one's personal library? Certainly. Does Lapis Lazuli House not have any books?"

"It does. On the second floor next to Mr. Flat's rooms is a library. He's banned me from entering."

"Yes, but I thought you had asserted your ownership and put Mr. Flat in his place?"

"I have," I argued. "My proof being that I now eat all my dinners in the dining room. However, the library was the *one* thing left to Archibald Flat when my great-aunt died. All the books in that library are his property."

"Does he read?"

"Oh, I expect not. How else would one remain so incredibly stupid? Forgive me. I mean— Well, actually, that is exactly what I mean. Me calling him stupid was less a reflection of his ability and more of the state in which he exists."

Now Mr. Pierce smiled. "The state in which he exists? So, as we supposedly abide in grace, Mr. Flat abides in stupidity?"

It was sound gospel to my ears.

"I believe he abides in grace *and* stupidity. I imagine it's not an uncommon human condition."

Mr. Pierce tilted his head, and his eyes crinkled around the edges. "No, I imagine not."

After a moment where we both contemplated such a thing, he said, "There are public libraries about. And what of your aunt's library?"

Need I explain my reading proclivities to every soul?

It seems I must.

I attempted a condensed version. "I cannot endure the borrowing of a book. I'm a deliberate reader, and I like to write notes in the margin."

"Notes in the margin?"

"Novels and novels' worth."

"You are a dangerous reader then."

"I would be. I *could* be—if my library consisted of more than four books. Perhaps I'll reread *Coriolanus*."

"No, no, no." And he was emphatic. "You can't only turn to Shakespeare, blessed as you think The Bard to be. Read something new. Read something you can argue with."

"You can argue with Shakespeare."

"No, you can't. Not really. Find something else."

"We've just gone over the entire catalogue of my library."

"Then read something from mine."

"Mr. Pierce, have you not listened to a single word I've just said?"

"I did. Ridiculous parameters you set for yourself. But here. If you must scribble in the margins. If you can only read what is your own." And he went over to a box, sorted through the contents, moved it aside, and searched another for whatever he was looking for.

It never occurred to me that Mr. Pierce would have books. It never occurred to me that he wouldn't. I'd just never paired the two. He comes and goes at all hours, is dedicated to his studio in between. The thought of him stopping long enough to read something other than a newspaper made me feel…something pleasant.

He pulled out a smallish brown volume, opened it up, flipped through a couple of pages, then closed it and walked over, placing it in my hands.

His natural gravity made the simple movement feel significant, as if he were handing me the Golden Fleece.

"Argue with this. It's yours."

Embarrassing and delightful. My life, in other words.

"I refuse to take your books," I said, even as my fingers may or may not have gripped the cover.

"I'm giving it to you."

I opened the front page and was met by an inscription.

Niall, my bold friend.
Rw. Emerson.

"I can't possibly accept this!" I waved the inscription in his face. "If I am to believe Rw. Emerson is, indeed, Ralph Waldo Emerson, who wrote"—I turned to the title page—'Self-Reliance', then I am not taking your personally inscribed copy!"

He shrugged it off. "I have two other copies, one of them also with an inscription."

Curiosity spoke for me next. "Oh? And what does that one say?"

"It says, 'Niall, you are stubborn and a fool. Rw. Emerson.'" He looked up, smiling. "I'd like to keep that one for myself."

"I really can't accept—"

Then he breathed out rather strongly and said, "Whenever I am in America, I feel so decidedly English. And whenever I am in England, I feel maddeningly American."

It was a singular pronouncement, and proof of his contamination to be sure, but I waited unspeaking—however unbelievable an action—for Mr. Pierce to explain why he made the statement.

He did.

"Emerson was a friend. I have three copies of this essay. I've read it and agreed with it and disagreed with it half a dozen times, if not more. So take this copy, Emma, and see what you can do with it. Don't be so bloody English. Scribble in the margins, underline, cross out, whatever you care or dare. But take the damn book."

My wide-eyed expression turned to a slow smile. "How very American of you, Mr. Pierce."

He groaned.

And I accepted the book.

August 3rd

I've told Parian and Agnes to take the day off. The last two weeks have been unbearable, and both of them—Agnes with grace and Parian with something less—have performed under miserable circumstances.

I will simply fend for myself when it comes to sustenance.

Agnes left a tray made up for Cousin Archibald in the pantry. All I have to do is boil water.

(The man will be lucky if I do not pour it on his ungrateful head.)

I've not yet begun to read "Self-Reliance." That is slated for this afternoon. I'm curious. Is it strange that I've never read any American works before?

No, answers a decent portion of my internal thought. You've all the literature you need between your two glorious islands.

However, there may be something to broadening the borders. Certainly not to gain citizenship in such a place, but a passport…?

Later

Oh dear. "Self-Reliance."

I had not read the first page in its entirety before disagreeing twice and ~~possibly~~ agreeing once.

This will be interesting, if not pleasant or comfortable.

~~Which sounds like a description of most Americans.~~

~~Perhaps that was unfair.~~

~~Perhaps not.~~

As soon as I opened the cover, Tybalt did something unexpected. He—having been asleep on my bed—flicked up his ears, lifted his head, stretched, then jumped from bed to desk.

"Have you come to witness my studies?" I asked.

In answer, he blinked. Then sat there, watching the entire time I read. The Tenant, it seems, has sent a spy.

Well.

Here is what he will report:

Notes on "Self-Reliance"
By one *Ralph Waldo Emerson,*
Friend and Critic of one *Niall Pierce*

"A man should learn to detect and watch that gleam of light which flashes across his mind from within, more than the lustre of the firmament of bards and sages. Yet he dismisses without notice his thought, because it is his."

That's a very democratic sentiment; however, it does not account for the number of absolute fools who have taken no time to learn how to think. Where is the shade of Socrates when one needs him? All this being said, I will follow the argument of this essay and see if the resolution passes muster, however outrageous his trust in the average mind.

Upon reviewing the above, I fear I am a snob.

Am I?

I would not have thought it.

For if I am a snob, what on earth could Aunt Eugenia be?

"There is a time in every man's education when he arrives at the conviction that envy is ignorance; that imitation is suicide..."

Violent, and interesting. So very interesting. There, Niall Pierce of the conflicted spirit, I give you this admission.

Later

Two pages in and I'm having a high dispute with myself and Mr. Emerson. I've looked, and there are thirty-nine pages to go.

Argument indeed. Mr. Pierce knew what he was speaking of.

I'm not certain tonight if I am a reader or a pugilist? Perhaps they are one and the same.

August 4th

There is no going back. I've closed the divide and thrown my lot in with the rebels across the sea. The pages of Emerson's essay are covered with notes. I've had to run out to the Reed and Rite for more ink as I've not only tattooed the margins but have scribbled several pages besides. (Admittedly, my abundant journal writing may hold a modicum of the blame for the expenditure of said ink.)

My mind has not enjoyed such conversation for a long while.

Shakespeare excepting.

Always Shakespeare excepting.

There are several memorable lines, but here are a few worth the assault to my journal:

God will not have his work made manifest by cowards.

I thought of Young Hawkes then.

Trust thyself: every heart vibrates to that iron string.

I believe even The Bard himself would have wished to write such a line. It is Bard-like, perhaps Bard-inspired?

Whoso would be a man, must be a nonconformist.

Noble sentiment, however, universal nonconformity could cause significant issues: Archibald Flat, exhibit A.

Your goodness must have some edge to it,—else it is none.

Ah, Mr. Emerson. Perhaps you are a man after my heart after all…

August 5th

Parian asked if he might attend church with me today. I was taken aback but answered that he might, as long as Agnes was at home to watch Cousin Archibald.

"She will remain at home," he answered. "She never attends church."

"No, she doesn't," I replied, thinking it was the last of what we had to say to one another.

And then Parian added, unnecessarily but entertainingly, "Agnes's mother told her to never listen to what is said in a London church, the heathen capital of the world."

Well!

Later

When Young Hawkes entered, he looked again as if he had been up all night. His hair askew, blue eyes serious about the business at hand. He read a large portion of Leviticus, and then once enough of the old guard had fallen asleep, he began his monthly round of poetry.

He does not go into the pompous claim of dramatics, but how that man can read verse. The Cambridge boys in the back even settled down, and every young woman leaned forward, letting the words fall over her like a spell.

Myself included.

After nearly half an hour, he read:

"What can I do to drive away
Remembrance from my eyes? for they have seen,
Aye, an hour ago, my brilliant Queen!
Touch has a memory. O say, love, say,
What can I do to kill it and be free
In my old liberty?"

But the way he said it! Honesty without affectation. *Touch has a memory*. In that moment, I could have sworn ghostly fingers lingered across the back of my neck.

He read the entire poem, Keats reincarnate, no longer dead in a lonely Italian tomb.

It was a haunting, a haunting of Hawkes as much as any of us.

A strange séance.

I almost felt the weight of Maxwell's eyes upon me.

I turned and…nothing. Only a chapel filled with every other ghost story to ever cross the lives of those present. Young Hawkes continued—with several lines I'd never thought to hear in a church—and then we came to the end. Spoken frankly without ornament, the words themselves carrying what his inflection did not.

> *"O, the sweetness of the pain!*
> *Give me those lips again!*
> *Enough! Enough! it is enough for me*
> *To dream of thee!"*

He finished, closed the volume before him, absently tapped it against his hand, glanced over the congregation holding our collective breath, and said, "Amen."

The final hymn was a token effort. Afterward, the congregants walked out of the church in a sort of daze.

When I turned towards Parian to say how remarkable it had been, he was asleep. Sound as a stone. Chin resting on his chest, mouth set in a frown.

Pearls before swine, I suppose.

I sighed. And woke him with a sharp elbow in his ribs.

Later

Today's interaction with one Niall Pierce was brief, and of the Pyramus and Thisbe variety:

HOW FARES EMERSON?

I can see that when I finish "Self-Reliance", you and I are going to have to battle it out.

I AWAIT THE FIRST VOLLEY.

August 6th

So very hot.

Abandoned by the cool winds of August.
The poets have failed me.
However, the Americans have not. Still reading.

A Few Additional Quotes from "Self-Reliance"

But perception is not whimsical, but fatal.

That there is a bit of genius.

The power men possess to annoy me I give them by a weak curiosity.

Ha!

Prayer is the contemplation of the facts of life from the highest point of view.

I would not claim to have achieved such lofty heights in my oblations. Mine are usually hasty thoughts from the very low place I occupy.

Another sort of false prayers are our regrets.

If this be the case, perhaps I'm more prayerful than I previously thought myself to be.

August 7th

I finished with Mr. Emerson this evening before dinner.

In truth, I have a creeping suspicion that I haven't finished *with* him at all.

However, I've made my first run at "Self-Reliance."

After I closed the volume, now absolutely littered with my notes, I realised I could eat a horse. Or something akin to the size of said animal. Taking the volume in hand, I wandered down (all) the stairs and into the front hall. From the aromas coming from the kitchen and the time of the clock, I knew dinner would be ready in short order.

I was going towards the kitchen when I noticed the studio door was open.

I poked my head into the room.

Uninvited.

Aunt Eugenia would flay me.

"Hello?" I called.

"Hello," came the reply. Then Mr. Pierce appeared from behind a large bureau he was arranging at the far end of the room.

"Good evening," I said, as if it were perfectly normal to accost unsuspecting photographers.

"That door is still open?" he asked.

"It is."

"My apologies, Miss Lion. Parian offered to fetch me a small hand saw, but he never returned. I've been too preoccupied to notice."

"How long ago was that?"

"A few hours?"

Parian. The model man to have in one's employ.

I apologised to Mr. Pierce and told him I certainly didn't mind the open door. "It's nice. It brings life to the house."

His smile when I said the word *life* looked like an anchor was tied to it.

If one were to follow his cues, one might think Mr. Pierce

something from another world entirely.

I did not ask him if he was a changeling grown.

Tempted as I was…

Rather, I said, "I finished Mr. Emerson's essay." And held it up triumphantly, waving it around a bit.

"And?"

"And I've plenty to say, so I suppose you will have to join me."

Mr. Pierce brushed his dark hair away from his forehead and rested a hand on the bureau he was adjusting. "Join you?"

"I am in hunt of sustenance. Dinner, as the St. Crispian's native would call it. Agnes reliably serves it in the dining room these days. I assume you've not eaten?"

He tapped his fingers on the side of the bureau and considered me. "I am not dressed for dinner."

He most certainly wasn't. Work trousers, old boots, sleeves of a faded white shirt rolled halfway up his forearms. No vest. No coat. Inviting a man dressed like a wandering labourer into my dining room is against All Rules of Genteel Existence. And if Bad Luck were to bring Aunt Eugenia to my door? A dear price would be exacted—that price probably being my head. (Aunt Eugenia does have a Herodian sense about her.) That being said, Aunt Eugenia hasn't stepped foot inside St. Crispian's in as many years as I've known her. I therefore deemed it safe and told him so.

"I'm your only company, Mr. Pierce. And you can see I'm in one of my old dresses, with no intention of changing for dinner, so come as you are."

It was then that Agnes appeared in the doorway, her eyes landing on Mr. Pierce, then skipping to me in mortification for having looked at him. "Dinner is ready, my lady."

"I'm no lady, Agnes. And will you set a second place? Mr. Pierce will be joining me."

Her wide eyes grew even wider, but she went without argument.

"She looks at me like I've drowned her cat," Mr. Pierce observed.

"You do seem to terrify."

"As I probably should," came his answer.

Before long we were in the dining room, sitting across from one another at the middle of the table, Mr. Pierce with his arm flung over the back of the chair beside him, unconsciously claiming the room in that wonderfully unaware way. With the book passed across the table between us, it did not take long before we were fully engrossed in our battle. Which wasn't a battle as much as it was a cross-examination.

Parian appeared—age of miracles in which we live—and served our food, while Mr. Pierce and I flung lines of Emerson across the table. Mr. Pierce enjoyed reading through all my slanted commentaries, furrowing his brows, deciphering my scribbles, grinning from time to time.

We ought to have hired a secretary to record our conversation, as I cannot do it justice. The pace was such that I only remember it in parts.

Like the first time he smirked at what I'd written.

"Are you laughing at me?"

"No," he said in a matter-of-fact manner as he turned a page and kept reading. "Yes. But in a delighted way."

"Oh, delighted is it?"

"Look at what you've written here. You challenge his notion of the self-helping man? Do you disagree? Does not the man who claims the steering of his own ship, who works hard, have '*all doors…flung wide?*'"

"Yes, wonderful," I answered. "The self-helping man. Fling open the doors. A parade for him. A medal from the Queen. However, I don't agree with the preceding statement that it is always foolish to '*sit down and cry for company*.' Sometimes we need an hour of woe before we can stand and deliver those '*rough electric shocks*' Emerson speaks of."

"You're speaking in particulars that his broader vision already accounts for."

"I am, but he does have a way of delivering his arguments that makes complete sense to disagree with one moment, only to agree the next. For example, he states on the same page we were just discussing that, '*As men's prayers are a disease of the will, so are their creeds a disease of the intellect.*'"

"Do you disagree?"

"I think to demand a person's prayers fall into any particular line is intrusive. As for creeds, I have found that sometimes the way through the maze is to enter into another's philosophy, take a look about, and then see oneself out on the other side. Is it foolishness to weigh and to measure various schools of thought? For how else is one to see?"

Mr. Pierce, crossing his arms and tilting his head to the side, asked, "You will defend your time in the classics then, however stale?"

"Unreservedly!" I may have banged the table with my fist. "I am not afraid to encounter these great men he speaks of—go fisticuffs with them if I must—to establish what I think of their philosophies. As for your Mr. Emerson, he seems as well versed in the classics as anybody, with all his quoting Caliph Ali."

It was then that Mr. Pierce truly laughed. Threw his head back and laughed. "He is a very educated man," Pierce said when he could manage the words. "And confident in speaking his contradictions, if they hammer away at truth."

"His truth? Your truth? Or The truth?"

"Isn't that the golden question?"

We went on like that for hours. Our food and drinks and dessert and tea appearing and disappearing as we battled our way through, only to find ourselves taking up each other's arguments in the end.

It felt as if it were…what can I say? A fission? An energy? All that mounting storm he carries about his person breaking in beautiful rain. And I thought to myself, This. This sort of battle, this kind of argument, this laughter when we realise we are saying the same thing—*this* is what I wish from life.

In the end, Mr. Pierce read the final lines of the essay: "*Nothing can bring you peace but yourself. Nothing can bring you peace but the triumph of your principles.*"

"I'm not certain I fully agree," I was compelled to answer, "but very well read."

He smiled.

I smiled.

How wonderful a thing to find one's friends.

August 8th

When I returned this afternoon, it was to the sound of voices in my drawing room. The tone, the smooth banter, the feeling that whoever was behind those doors was very pleased with themselves, all struck me as familiar.

As Parian was nowhere to be found, I opened the door.

"There she is!"

"Hello, mad thing!"

Sitting in my drawing room, one on the green sofa, one in the pink chair, were the blessed banes of all existence, Oliver and Phineas Brookstone.

"Two scoundrels in one day," I said. "What luck."

They stood, and we exchanged kisses before I sat with Phineas on the sofa.

"Due to Arabella's report, I'm surprised to see you in the country," I told them. "I thought you'd fled the threat of matrimony for a life on the Continent?"

Phineas and Oliver smiled in tandem, looking very privileged and very English. Light brown hair, green eyes, rather more sun-kissed than usual. Identical. Somewhat disturbing.

"We've missed the first rash of engagements, and all the desperates have found fiancés, so Mother deemed it safe to return." Phineas crossed his legs and leaned back on the sofa. "She needed us to be present for some event or other."

"And what does she think of you looking so hale and hearty?"

"Mother thinks we're splendid," Oliver drawled. "Father, on the other hand, carries a staunch belief that it is un-English and has banned all riding until our pallor is translucent, with touches of red. He's very patriotic, the old man. Thinks it our British duty to look sickly."

Well.

"Did you happen upon my cousin Damian while abroad?"

Oliver glanced at Phineas. There was a silent communication, and then they turned to face me, offering a simultaneous "No."

What, I wondered, was Damian up to now? As they did not wish to divulge the information, I pressed on. "Will you be staying long in London?"

"In and out, mad thing," Phineas said. "In and out."

"But now, Emma." Oliver sounded quite serious. "Arabella tells us you're here for good. Do you intend to stay in London *all* year?"

I smiled. "Lapis Lazuli House is my home. Where else should I want to be?"

"It's rather sooty year-round, a bit drab, don't you think?" Phineas asked, lifting an eyebrow.

"I've no idea. It will be my first winter."

Their response was one of nonverbal pity. Then Oliver sighed. "Time to do the dirty deed, Phineas."

Phineas, appearing resigned, dug in his pocket and withdrew a familiar peach envelope.

A compulsory groan escaped my throat.

"We've just been to see Arabella and were asked to be messengers by your aunt. Here you are. We apologise for facilitating the imposition of social horrors, Em."

He placed the envelope in my hand.

We all stared at it a moment before I, lifting a determined chin, opened said peach envelope.

"Do read it to us, old sport," Oliver smiled.

"Yes, do. Her insults are simply the best."

"The two of you are terrible." A thing I believe they took as a compliment, and so I clarified, "I am not going to read my personal correspondence aloud."

Phineas made a squeak on his way to a laugh. "Oh, she read aloud as she was composing. In the Second drawing room, I might add. We've been demoted from the First."

"Why am I convinced you deserve the demotion?"

I opened the letter and began to read.

Emma,

You are to report to Spencer House on the twenty-third to

prepare for the Duchess of Bedford's Ball. I had no intention of inviting you, as it is an Event far beyond Your Status, however tied to me by Blood you may be. But the lazy louts who delivered this missive, namely Phineas and Oliver Brookstone, will be in attendance.

At which point Phineas began to laugh.

As this is a Crucial Night for Arabella, we can't have those fools bungling any of my plans…

At which point Oliver also began to laugh.

They are idiots of every kind. You see my dilemma…

"We do," inserted the twins simultaneously.

I have ordered Madame Tasset to remake one of Arabella's nicest gowns to your specifications so you will not embarrass us by your appearance. It will be finished by the twenty-third. If you do not keep those Brookstone boys AWAY from Arabella, I will punish you by any means necessary.

Come to tea on Friday.

Your Aunt

I looked up at the boys. "She makes the two of you sound like the plague. What in heaven's name did you do?"

Oliver's smirk was the nonverbal answer to Phineas saying, "We both indicated we'd like to marry Arabella, just to rile the old girl up."

I felt Aunt Eugenia's frigid chill creep around my heart. "You didn't."

"We expect to be relegated to the Third drawing room within the month. It should go over well at the club."

Bold, foolhardy, and a touch mad, going against Aunt Eugenia for entertainment's sake, but the Brookstone twins have always set their expectations high.

It wasn't long before they were on their way out. "We're going to Blackman's to start rumours that Phineas and I are looking at wedding rings," Oliver said, kissing me on the cheek. "See you on the twenty-third, Emma."

August 9th

Dr. Fairchild came by today to assess the state of Cousin Archibald's leg.

It was a gruesome affair.

Archibald is not yet ready to be up and refuses to let Parian bathe him. The room, therefore, is beginning to smell rather terrible.

The good doctor appeared not to notice and said he thought that in two weeks' time Archibald could begin putting a small amount of weight on his leg each day.

"You're trying to snap it right off," declared Archibald. "You're in league with the witch!"

Fairchild had the good grace to appear confused, although his few visits have established that all negative sentiments are to be sent in my direction.

"You are fortunate, Mr. Flat," Fairchild said gracefully. "Miss Lion and Parian have provided excellent care."

"It's only part of her grand scheme!" came Archibald's utterance, spittle and all, in return.

"Heavens, I am impressive," answered I. "I didn't realise I was a part of any *grand* schemes."

The good doctor resisted his smile until we were in the hall outside the bedroom. It was then I had the pleasure to hear something I've never heard in my life.

Emma M. Lion records a High Compliment

"You are a saint, Miss Lion," Fairchild stated, and without irony. "Of the First Order."

Let it be marked.

I, Emma M. Lion, am a Saint.

Of the First Order.

I'm rather impressed with myself. To be a saint of any order is a fine thing, even an enviable one. Yet I would imagine there are a fair number of those. But to be a saint of the first order?

The man must not have heard about the debacle at The Cleopatra.

As we were descending the stairs, he said something a bit odd.

"Miss Lion, I gather Niall Pierce is your tenant?"

"Yes," I replied. "My famously patient tenant."

Fairchild cleared his throat. "Do you know him well?"

I was taken aback. It was said with an *air*.

"Everything I do know gives me cause to celebrate my success in acquiring him," was my loyal reply.

Fairchild nodded, and when we arrived in the hall—Agnes bringing his hat, practicing a rather ornate curtsy, then disappearing back into the kitchen—he cleared his throat in a doctoral way.

"Mr. Pierce is a fine man. A very fine man. More than most would know."

"Why do I get the feeling you are covering another thought entirely?"

"No, no," he answered. "Only, however good a man, there are flaws to every nature."

I don't pretend to claim Mr. Pierce a saint. (I reserve that distinction for myself. See above commentary.) However, I thought Mr. Fairchild spoke out of turn.

I roused a defence.

"Doctor Fairchild, Niall Pierce has been a good tenant and come to my aid on many fronts."

"I'm sure he has. That's very like him. Don't misunderstand me, Miss Lion. Niall Pierce is one of the finest men I know. Of all the tenants you could have, he is of the best."

"That's just what I think." I smiled.

"Is his leg still bothering him a great deal?"

Another sideways if not odd question. "He never mentions it. Perhaps you ought to ask him yourself."

"Hmm." But the doctor looked unconvinced.

After I let Fairchild out, I stood a few minutes behind the closed door.

August 10th

Tea with Aunt Eugenia and Arabella.

After a round lecture on the Behaviours I Must Display at the Duchess of Bedford's ball, we were ordered to sit quietly, contemplating our small place in the universe. Arabella broke the humble period of reflection by saying, "I've had a letter from Damian. He sends his love."

Before I could answer aught, Aunt Eugenia pronounced, "Do not speak his name. I am not acknowledging I have a son at present."

"Oh?" I asked with a glance of co-conspiracy. "I take it he's not returning for the Duchess of Bedford's ball on the twenty-third?"

"He most certainly is not." And with a huff and a sweep, Aunt Eugenia left us alone.

I gave Arabella a knowing look. "If Damian sent his love, I'll eat my own hand."

"You're right," Arabella admitted. "I made that up. He was asking if you or I had anything to sell, as Mama has cut his allowance and he's running low on funds."

Now that certainly sounds like my dear cousin.

"But Damian is now Lord Spencer. Aren't they his funds?"

Arabella gave me a look as if to enquire if I'd ever met her mother.

Touché.

I did ask Arabella if she knew why Damian was in Aunt Eugenia's bad graces.

"I believe he's been running through the streets of Rome after an Italian girl. Mama does not approve."

"I should say not," I replied. "However, if he married an Italian, they would have beautiful children."

Arabella lifted a lazy shoulder in a shrug. "Mama doesn't approve of beauty that isn't wholly English."

An English tea is such a partisan affair.

August 11th

Dear Emma,

There are more counts in Italy than one has time—or desire—to paint. In desperation I've turned to landscapes. I'm going to be coming home with more than I can sell, so please do me a favour. Go to my studio, see all is in order, and pick two or three paintings you like of those leaning against the wall.

I've just turned down my seventh proposal of the summer. Italy is good for my confidence and bad for my vanity.

Yours, with affection,

Saffronia March

August 12th

Young Hawkes, once again, looked as if he had been up all night. He delivered a sermon on Aaron and Hur holding up the arms of Moses. I noticed the young gentlemen along the back row were unusually quiet, hanging their heads and giving each other sheepish grins.

However, the real gem of the day came after the sermon, in form of whispered rumour. By all accounts, The Roman—my dear elusive shade—has been seen on Whereabouts Lane.

Reportedly, Mrs. Ivy Ale saw him a few nights back.

How delightful.

A comfort *Julius Caesar* has failed to drive him away.

It is almost dark, and I've taken up watch at the half window of my garret. This gloaming hour seems more melancholy and beautiful on the Sabbath.

I have taken the entitled *Meaning of Flowers* from the shelf in the breakfast room, and have been leafing through. Beautifully done. I especially like the dandelion.

My half window is open, and so is the half belonging to,

Latin name: The Tenant

Common name: Niall Pierce

Botanical family: Photographer

I know this because I braved leaning out the window. It is open!

If we wished, we could pass one another necessities.

A piece of cake, for example. Or a dictionary.

August 13th

I've just taken Agnes with me to Miss March's house.

After convincing the housekeeper that we were there on the errand of Miss March herself—I produced the letter as evidence—I led Agnes up to the studio and said, "We're here to find a few treasures for my walls. But keep an eye out to see if there is anything you would care to hang in the kitchen."

And I began the hunt, leaving Agnes to do the same.

Miss March's studio is the right amount of order and chaos, a perfectly balanced universe. Things are ordered, but in a disordered way. There is colour everywhere, mostly in the form of paint on the wooden floor and the abandoned easels. The windows are tall and clear, allowing good northern light, and there are piles of studies and brushes.

The canvases were leaning against the walls.

Beautiful landscapes, figures with clever faces, gardens and architecture… Such an interesting array. She is very good. Some of her paintings are their own kind of genius. So say the critics. So said my father.

I selected a painting of a garden, one architectural piece, and a solitary figure near a window, deciding to give these three a chance to haunt my garret. When I looked towards Agnes, she was clutching a canvas to her chest.

"Did you find something you like?" I asked.

"Very much so, Miss Lion," she replied almost reverently.

"Wonderful. Hang it wherever you like."

And between the two of us, we carried our four paintings home.

Later

I walked into the kitchen just now, to ask Agnes if there was anything she needed me to purchase while at the Reed and Rite, only to find myself staring into the eyes of Islington, Duke of.

"Agnes! What in the world is this?" I cried. She rushed from the pantry and followed my stare to the portrait now hanging in my kitchen.

While it is not the flesh-and-blood variation of Islington I've come to know, he still looked at me with some disapproval.

"You said I could take whichever I liked!" Agnes whined like a trapped fox. She sounded terribly embarrassed.

"Yes, I did. I just didn't expect…"

Flushed a full crimson, Agnes mounted a feeble defence. "When I saw this one, it made me think of great houses, and all the pictures they have of noble people, and—and—and—and I thought it wouldn't be so very… Would it?"

I sighed and looked at Islington again.

From what I could tell, the painting wasn't wholly finished, but in a pleasing way—some broader strokes around the edges, the colouring not so rich as most completed works. It appears to be a study for a larger portrait. Islington sitting in a chair, disapproving by nature, yes, but also looking like he was doing his best not to intimidate. He was, of course, failing miserably at it.

Agnes, silently suffering as I studied our unexpected guest, deserved a reprieve, and so I said, "It's just right, Agnes. It is not uncommon to have a likeness of one's friends about." And my smile allowed her to do the same, lips still quivering, her eyes threatening the worst bout of young tears I've yet seen on display at Lapis Lazuli House. "Only keep him in the kitchen. I don't think the duke would care to be sitting anywhere else."

She gave the portrait a private smile as if she'd gotten away with a lovers' tryst, then asked if I would like my tea.

I accepted.

Resigned to my fate.

August 14th

I was returning from the park an hour ago, walking down Whereabouts, when I encountered Mr. Pierce walking—or rather, slightly limping—up Whereabouts. Our meeting resulted in an invitation to see his nearly completed studio.

It's beautiful, and I am somewhat envious.

It came about in a friendly sort of way.

First, general niceties were exchanged.

"Good evening, Mr. Pierce."

"Such as it is, Miss Lion."

"How goes the studio? Are you almost open for business?"

"I believe so," he answered. He sounded rather than looked pleased. His expression was tightened around the corners, with pain, I presume.

Second, came an invitation.

"Would you like to see the state of things?" he enquired.

"Of course!"

"I'll meet you inside," he said while fishing his key from his pocket.

We approached our respective doors, both our locks catching at the same moment before we twisted them again, pushed in, and closed our doors behind us in unison.

Parian was coming down the stairs, a tray of abandoned tea things in his hands.

"How are you, Parian?" I tried to be congenial. "Was your day off refreshing?"

He lifted that pointed nose of his, gave me a side eye disproportionate to my question, and walked down the hall towards the kitchen stairs. If the man wasn't looking after Cousin Archibald, I might have sacked him. Seeing, however, as he is performing such a heroic feat, I left him to it.

Looking through the mail on the side table—a bill from the grocer is all—I waited until I could hear Mr. Pierce in the studio, then I took off my hat and my gloves, walked across the hall, and reached to knock on the studio door just as he opened it.

"Come in," he said. "The evening light will show it off to advantage, I think."

It most certainly did.

The Atmosphere that is Mr. Niall Pierce has been beautifully transferred to his studio. The result, a strange intoxication. The same feeling one has when watching a storm from a covered portico. The blue walls mimic his height, the rich hue complementing the red curtains, which he keeps tied back. The plum sofa is near two of the windows, but pulled away a few feet, with a large rug—from some far-flung place—before it. A brown leather chair sits to one side of the sofa, creating an L between them. In the centre of the rug is a low table, the perfect size to put one's feet on if alone, the ideal height for a tray of tea things if with company.

There are a few framed photographs hung, and many more leaning against the walls, awaiting their placement. All black and white save one, a softly coloured photograph of some exotic land, with palms trees, strange architecture, and foreign horizon line. My credenza—the fig leaf credenza—is below it, and there are a few periodicals, a lamp, and a plant arranged on top.

Speaking of plants, he has two or three trees potted and placed artfully around the room, mostly near the windows. I was and am completely charmed by them.

There is a worktable in the centre of the studio, towards the south wall. And at the far end, in the corner left of the door to Lapis Lazuli Minor, are two large bureaus painted black which look to be for storage. The space to the right of the door, closer to the window, is left open.

I asked him if he would take portraits there, and he said, "Yes, though I can move anything around if needs be."

"Those rolled-up items in the corner? Are they your backdrops?"

Mr. Pierce looked pained. "Unfortunately, yes."

"They cannot be so very bad," I countered.

He merely grunted.

We were in the midst of the grand tour when Agnes appeared in the doorway.

"I've taken Mr. Flat his dinner, Miss Lion."

"Thank you, Agnes. Did he try and bite you today?"

"Yes, but I was faster."

"How is Mr. Flat?" Mr. Pierce asked me, his voice only half concern.

"Foul mood, but still unable to rise from his bed. A blessing to us all." I then said to Agnes, "If you've the food prepared already, I'll take my dinner now."

Agnes curtsied in response. I've no idea why.

"Will you go up to change then, Miss?" she asked.

As she knows I've never changed (with the exception of the ill-fated night we'd invited Mr. Pierce to dinner), I thought it an odd question.

"I do not often change for dinner in my own home, do I, Agnes?"

"No, Miss. Only my mother says that a true lady always changes, even in death."

"Even in death? As in, when one has died? How remarkable. I've thought the ladies of society to be less capable than that."

Poor girl. I shouldn't tease.

"I meant the deaths of their nearest and dearest."

"Ah."

And from the corner of my eye, I could see Mr. Pierce turn away with an escaped smile.

"I will not change this evening, Agnes, but I thank you for giving me a measure to work towards."

She curtsied again and left.

I looked towards Mr. Pierce, who was considering a few of his unhung photographs and looking about the room.

"Would you like to join me for dinner, Mr. Pierce? I wouldn't insist you change, not even in death."

"Thank you for your invitation, Miss Lion," he said, his eyes turning to me only after he had spoken. "I've a dinner appointment this evening. One I must change for, regretfully."

"What a pillar of society you are."

"My role is to be a novelty of society, Miss Lion. Never a pillar."

I grinned. "Even better."

When I returned to the garret, after a dinner I did not change for, I found a dead snake coiled up in the corner of my rug. Tybalt was napping on the chair, and when I cried out in surprise, he opened one eye as if to say, "You're welcome."

Then he went back to sleep.

August 15th

I've had no response from Evelyn to my letter regarding Maxwell's burial.

I allow it's only been eighteen days.

But surely that is enough to compose a simple letter, i.e.,

> *Emma,*
>
> *Yes, we are bringing Maxwell home.*
> *On such and such a date.*
> *Come for the service.*
>
> *Evelyn*

Or possibly,

> *Emma,*
>
> *No, father is a tight-fisted flint.*
> *He will not brook the expense.*
> *Maxwell is never coming home.*
>
> *Evelyn*

Neither seems beyond one's ability, even if that one is inward thinking, cruel, and egotistical.

~~Steady now, Emma. Don't be such a humbug.~~

Humbug as you like. It's awful he hasn't written.

Perhaps Evelyn has changed his personality *complètement* and, instead of a selfish creature, has transformed into an industrious soul who hasn't time to reply as he's too busy feeding the poor or teaching orphans to read.

My doubts of such a thing are robust.

Later

As my thoughts this morning were too dark for August, I decided to do a good deed. If Victorian morality cannot sustain me, what will? And so I wandered into Cousin Archibald's den of lies, foul odours, and deceits.

"Is there anything I can bring you, Cousin? Perhaps a pastry from Everett's?"

There was not, as it happens, anything he wanted from my tainted hand.

This message was delivered with many profanities and a slipper thrown in my general direction.

August 16th

I'm sitting in the half window of my garret, Mother's Bible turned open to the book of Revelation.

> *And I looked, and behold a pale horse: and his name that sat on him was Death, and Hell followed with him…*

I blame Mr. Pierce.

He referenced it after an unintended tea this afternoon.

A thing which happens. I defy anyone to live without the occasional.

Unintended teas, I mean. Not Mr. Pierce quoting gothic scripture.

That is a rare bird, not likely to be seen again.

Although with a voice like his, I'm inclined to think his reading of any ancient text would hit the mark…

I digress.

It was my clumsiness which led us to the book of Revelation—I'm not often clumsy—but it was Agnes's lack of control which brought the entire scene about.

For Agnes had made too many scones.

~~As if there is such a thing.~~

There may be such a thing, but I doubt anyone has ever seen it.

So I—generosity itself—stopped by my former-salon-turned-studio and invited Mr. Pierce to join me.

He accepted.

I meant for us to have tea in the drawing room, but as he was busy cleaning his camera equipment, I waited, bothering him with questions regarding the various pieces to which he was attending. It was then that Agnes arrived at the door of the studio, tea tray in hand.

"Oh no, Agnes, we will take it in the drawing room. No need to clutter up Mr. Pierce's studio."

Mr. Pierce was quick to say that he wouldn't mind, and would she be so good as to set the tray on the low table before the sofa?

She did, and then scurried out.

Mr. Pierce came and sat.

Tea was had.

I didn't say much, beyond asking a good many questions. (That sentence looks contradictory, but it isn't. At least by my definition.) My questions regarded the photographs hanging about the room. As I enquired as to their history, he reminisced, told me stories—although I suspect he stepped around the facts just enough to keep most of the history obscured.

One photograph was of a small pond, a few men and a woman standing at the water's edge speaking with one another. The photograph in and of itself was beautifully captured, especially the light off the water in the distance. The men had their backs to the photographer, but the woman, in all white, was glancing over her shoulder. As she was in motion, her face was the only part of the photograph not in focus. It was not as sweeping or grand as his other works, but there was an energy about it, an elemental simplicity.

"Where was that taken?"

"America. Massachusetts. That gentleman there? There is your Mr. Emerson."

"Really?"

I was pleased to see the back of the man I'd been arguing with.

"And what took you to America in the first place?" I asked.

I wasn't aware of Mr. Pierce having taken a particularly long breath, but his exhale was slow and lasted a small eternity. "There are many wars, Miss Lion. Not all of them are fought with rifles."

And he stood and went back to his work while I, at my leisure despite his evasion, finished my cup of tea. It seems I'm acclimatising to his weather.

After I'd finished, I looked at the number of things strewn and piled around the studio and offered to help.

"There must be something I can do."

Mr. Pierce pointed towards a stack of boxes. "Those need to go in that bureau there, the one on the left. The shelves were custom-built to house them. Labels out, if you please."

The boxes themselves also appeared custom; an irregular shape, flatter and longer than usual, and each was labelled on the side, some with names, some with dates. I set about ordering them as best I could—where, for example, would one place a box entitled *MOVEMENT STUDIES*? There were years, *1864–1865*. (The final years of the American Civil War, I presume?) Then labels such as *AFTER APPOMATTOX, PASSAGE, DAMASCUS, LOST ROADS, NEW YORK 1874–75, ASHANTI, SOUTH AFRICA*, et cetera.

It required an amount of personal honour to keep from turning my back and opening the boxes. It would be a violation. As if I were taking the lid off of Mr. Pierce's soul and rummaging around to see what I might find.

Alas.

And now we come to the clumsy action the entire day is now pinned on. I, making stacks of like boxes, turned too quickly and sent a box toppling over, the lid abandoning ship as soon as it was able and the photographs sliding onto the ground.

"Miserable fortune," I said as Mr. Pierce glanced my way then came over to help. As I reached for the box, intending to shuffle the black and white images back in their place, I saw the label written on the side.

AFGHANISTAN 1880.

The now familiar handwriting stating the year and place where a significant part of my future was obliterated by gunshot.

It was not, I should say, ideal.

If I were the heroine of a novel, I would have felt my heart clutch, the misery of what happened all those miles away causing me to freeze, perhaps closed my eyes tightly, hands shaking, feeling all the difficult corners of loss.

But I am not the heroine of a novel. I am flesh, blood—interesting enough on occasion, with dull edges here and there, living a life of the expected and the unexpected, the wanted and the worst of the unwanted.

So, as I stood there holding the emptied box in my hands, the photographs spilled about the floor, I knew I had to keep it all at bay. Force a measure of matter-of-fact thinking on the moment.

On the floor was the war where he died. The very year. And I was feeling somewhat blank. Realising this, a thousand questions went through my mind. Am I getting better? Is three years of grief enough payment? Does the heart not always have to wear black? Is this a sign I am moving forward in the way Arabella keeps insisting I must? Am I simply mistaking paralysis for healing? Will all of these questions seem foolish when hindsight has entered the messy equation?

Mr. Pierce understood what was happening, what we were both staring at. And I thank him for not saying anything before I did.

"Do you think I should look at them?" I asked with strange, academic consideration. "You've offered before. Do you think I should know what it was?"

He tilted his head forward, the corners of his mouth turned down, saying nothing.

"Do you think them unfit for a woman to see?" I added.

"They are meant to be seen by all. I make no distinction."

Yet he hesitated.

I waited until he walked around me, balanced on the balls of his feet, and began to carefully gather the photographs, recovering their order. When he finally spoke, it was with honesty. "These are not pleasant pictures, Miss Lion. They are not sonnets to the glories of warring for God and country."

"I guessed as much."

"You will suffer for it. You will see the death of your Maxwell for what it was."

"I know," I said.

I didn't, though.

And thinking back on his expression, he understood that.

"Other photographers were angry at what I dared capture. Blood and mangle and broken bodies." He stood up then, holding the photographs. "Death is here in my hands."

This was the point I ought to have realised my numb detachment as a form of denial.

That I wouldn't be able to see them and say, "Well, for the glories of war…"

"Do you still wish to look?" he pressed.

"Would you?" was all I thought to say. "If you were me?"

"Yes." It came swiftly. And earnestly. "I would want to understand. However painful the price."

I took in the expression on his face, warned myself that this was a haunted man, and then gave a quick nod so I could not take it back.

"Sit," he ordered. I crossed the room and sat down on the sofa. He followed, and I pushed the tea things aside so there might be room for the photographs. Once he placed them before me, he sat down on the arm of his leather chair and crossed his arms. "Afghanistan," he said.

I leaned forward and just managed to grip my hands around the stack of photographs, bringing them to rest on my lap.

The first images were of soldiers standing about their tents, encampments seen from the tops of hills, men of an Afghan family gathered together. And then there was an image of a body lying alone in a field, the lines of a British uniform for the desert unfamiliar. The body was twisted, sprawled. No nobility, only an unnatural reminder of who this young man may have been. His face was turned away.

I blinked.

"Those are the only pleasant images you will see," Mr. Pierce stated.

Still looking at the dead soldier, I acknowledged him wordlessly, then I moved to the next photograph.

My flinch must have been visible.

There was a line of soldiers on their backs, hands above their heads.

The next was of a single soldier. He looked strange. "His hand," I said. "His chest?"

Mr. Pierce's answer was not pleasant. "Bloated. I found him a few days after he was killed. He had been missing. Don't look at the next—"

But I already had. The same soldier from a different angle, a misshapen face in clear view, the eyes—what was left of them—open. It was an instinct to place my hand over the face, closing my own eyes to the grotesque mockery of a stolen life. But this did not take the image away.

I did not know the young man in the photograph, yet all I could think was *Maxwell.*

"Are there more like this?" I asked.

"Yes."

I knew I should not have gone on, but I looked at the next image, and the next. A pile of bodies beside a wagon. Graves dug, soldiers waiting for burial. One hollowed corpse in his uniform. Eyes wide. Lips pulled tight in the malformation of death. A medal was pinned to his chest.

It taunted me as much as the blank gaze of the soldier.

All of Maxwell's medals were sent home to Barrows Edge.

I set the photographs aside. Ashamed for having looked. Ashamed for having to look away.

Mr. Pierce discerned my thoughts. "The damnation is on the heads of the leaders of nations. It is their shame—only ours if we subscribe to the imperialism which sanctions such things."

Mr. Pierce took the photographs away, placed them in their box, resettled the lid, and put it inside the bureau. A story to shelve, miles from our living, breathing lives.

Did they put Maxwell in a coffin, hastily nailed together? Or was it just a hole in the ground?

I kept seeing the faces, the malformed corpses, and I lifted my fingers to my closed eyes, as if the act could dismiss the phantoms I very well knew I had brought upon myself.

"Are you all right, Emma?"

I did not fully register in that moment that he'd used my given name, that the doors of Appropriate Formality—all honesty demands I acknowledge that was thrown out weeks ago—had been opened with little likelihood they would be able to close again.

No, I was focused on the content of his question. I wasn't all right.

I was horrified. I was angry. I told him so in as many words. As he nodded, a strange light came into his eyes.

"Good," he answered sharply. "Be angry. Be terribly, bloody angry. Better fury than sorrow."

I blinked at him. In all the years of loss, no one had ever told me that was acceptable.

Before I could answer anything, he stood. "Come on. Let's go. Gather whatever you need. You and I are going for a long walk."

"A walk?" I clarified, as if it were an easy word to misunderstand.

"A walk," he replied. "Bring your anger with you. Fuel it, wrestle with it, burn with it. And we will walk the streets of London until you can manage it, or at least keep it banked. I'm not abandoning you with those images in your head. I'll not have you return to where you were a fortnight ago."

It was…

Well, my grief felt more considered than it had since Maxwell died. As if I were given a weapon to fight the unbearable.

"A walk then," I answered.

He turned away, crossed the room, and opened the door leading to Lapis Lazuli Minor. "Wear good shoes," he said over his shoulder.

I wore good shoes.

My old brown boots that had seen me through three years of caring for Cousin Matilde, dragon in residence.

We walked down Whereabouts Lane and crossed King Henry's Road. After that I didn't bother with the direction. Just took whatever cues he gave and walked and walked. I did not ask for Mr. Pierce's arm, nor did he offer. He kept a long stride despite his limp—it could not have been comfortable—and it took more than a little effort to keep the pace. I expected him to slow before long. He did not.

People and carriages and horses moved in the periphery of our thoughts, but they remained apart from us, like a painted landscape and Mr. Pierce the cloud moving across it. I did not want to think of the photographs, yet I made my mind remember what I had seen. Trusting Mr. Pierce understood war more than I, I took his advice: when the sour anger rose in my chest, I grabbed hold of it, forced myself to keep hold—thoughts and memories and newspaper clippings running through all of it. It was not surprising that it ended with Evelyn. The bitterness on my tongue as I thought of my unanswered letter.

We were nearing the buildings of Parliament, and I glanced up at Mr. Pierce. His eyes were dark as he glared at Westminster.

"If you'd like to spit, I promise not to tell," I said.

His answering smile was black, but he turned his eyes from Parliament towards the steady calm of the Thames. "They don't even deserve the effort."

Nothing more was said until we were crossing the river. "Mr. Pierce, if you do not slow your pace, even a small amount, I am pushing you into the water without a second thought. Your legs are longer than mine, despite—"

Emma.

It was unthinking. And a relief I caught myself.

Good manners demand that one should not jest about a man's crippled state before he does.

He gave no indication he registered the moment, said nothing. But we both knew what had been omitted.

He did, however, slow down, taking his hands from his pockets and removing his hat.

Having established a pace I could endure at length, we continued on, leaving respectable London for places I'd never been and likely wouldn't have gone without his company.

As our afternoon walked through the doorway of evening, we found ourselves on the northern edge of Primrose Hill. My feet hurt, blisters forming—forming? formed!—on my left heel. My hem was filthy. Sweat ran down my back between my shoulders.

I was worn through.

We sat down on a bench with a view that allowed the London skyline to rise above the trees.

I took a long breath. "Have you *many* friends, Mr. Pierce?"

"Why do you ask?"

He looked, if I am any judge, as tired as I, and was trying to massage the muscles of his injured leg without me seeing.

I pretended not to notice and answered, "Because if wearing them to a senseless exhaustion is your way of giving them aid, I'd not think it likely you remain in their good graces for very long."

He grinned then, and I felt triumphant. "I've far worse faults that drive them away. But the true ones have stayed. Despite the brutal marches I put them through."

"Glad to hear it."

A few familiar faces walked past. We smiled, the men tipped hats, Mr. Pierce gave the barest acknowledgement, shifting so as to be more comfortable, keeping his grimace from his mouth but not his eyes.

I could feel myself mimicking the expression and took it upon myself to deliver the man home to the privacy of his own garret.

"We should return now, I think. Having left Agnes and Parian alone with Cousin Archibald for hours might possibly have resulted in a crime."

He nodded and stood, his eyes a bright silver despite the creases about their edges. It left me without any room to complain about my blistered feet. However much I wanted to cry out.

We limped out of the park and down Whereabouts Lane, the evening growing dark in the purple of any number of summer evenings.

As we came to the door of Lapis Lazuli Minor, I turned to thank him, but he was staring past me intensely.

"Are you all right, Mr. Pierce?"

He blinked, then shifted his gaze to me, his eyes holding mine fast. "Do you despise me, Emma?"

It was not the question I'd expected to hear.

"Despise you?" I asked. "Why would I? Why *should* I?"

"You know what I am. What I do." He looked pained. "I am a man chained to dark places. I follow the pale horse."

I knew the reference immediately.

It swept through me with a hollow feeling.

"*And I looked, and behold a pale horse: and his name that sat on him was Death, And Hell followed with him…*" I quoted, strange words to speak aloud.

The weight of his person, so companionable before, felt like a force of another kind.

For one irrational moment I wondered exactly what stood before me.

But then a bird call came.

A few young boys ran across the street.

And the shade that stalked him—whatever it was—passed. I was simply standing with Niall Pierce, who had forced the pain inside of me to walk until it had collapsed into the soles of my feet.

"I do not despise you," I answered. "I am sorry for what you've seen."

He dismissed that with a shrug, then turned to grip the railing. Still, he did not go inside.

I took a breath and steered us away from the topic with whatever my mind could grasp. It landed on the unspoken and unexpected transgression of the day.

"Twice now you have used my given name. I thought you'd decided against such rash action?"

He sat down on the stairs, making the sound of a pained hiss. "Even if I wished the appropriate formality, I don't think it likely. When I first said that would be best, we had yet to eat dinner together, rescue your ridiculous cousin, speak seriously of a neighbourhood ghost I still doubt exists—no, let me finish—nor had we yet claimed joint ownership of a cat. To say nothing of every other thing that has transpired since I moved into your bewitched house. At this juncture, it feels disingenuous calling you Miss Lion. At least in private."

"Well said. I suppose it was inevitable that any formality between us was doomed to fall victim to the law of diminishing returns."

"Law of diminishing—" He made an amused sound. "Emma it is then. In private."

"Am I therefore given permission to call you Niall? In private?"

"Niall, or Pierce. Whatever suits you. My friends call me either."

"Then it's settled. I'll use them both to great effect."

He eyed me for a long moment, then, without any warning, extended his hand.

Thinking about it after, I realised that for all our messages between walls, we'd never yet touched one another. I might be deluding myself now that there was a significance as I removed my right glove and extended my hand in return.

Now I'm sounding foolish.

But when we shook hands, it was…well, there was a jolt.

Like touching lightning.

We both started and pulled our hands away, his face registering the surprise mine must have shown. I fumbled to replace my glove as he said, "I should go in. I've a dinner appointment."

I grimaced without meaning to, pity for his leg. But his expression warned me away from any verbal concern.

"Thank you for what you've done. I'm—I am much more fighting fit than I would be otherwise."

"Of course," he answered. "You won't be too…unsettled?"

I replied honestly. "I've no idea. But if I am, I'll simply bother you, once you've returned."

"No bother, Emma."

Then he left, doing his best to walk evenly up the steps of Lapis Lazuli Minor.

When I entered the front door, I was met by a fretful Agnes.

"I wondered if he'd done you in, Miss! But I could'na think of where he'd have put your body!"

I believe my face showed mild disappointment. "Agnes. Really! Anyone knows the river is as good a place as any."

And now it's past midnight, my nightdress is stained with ink, and I'm feeling apprehensive about sleep. I'm halfway through the book of Revelation with all of its horses, and finding little comfort there.

I wonder how soon Niall Pierce will be home, pacing on the other side of the wall.

August 17th

Arabella invited me to tea this afternoon.

The conversation went like so:

"You look quite awful, Emma. What have you been doing with yourself?"

"I've stayed up half the night reading the book of Revelation."

"Why on earth would one ever do such a thing?"

I sighed. "Because I live with a tormented man."

"Live with?"

"Live next to."

"You are a scandal, my dear Irishman's daughter."

"Is the daughter dear or the Irishman?"

"The Irishman."

I always suspected as much.

Alas.

As I was leaving, I was met by Aunt Eugenia's maid, holding a dreaded peach envelope.

Emma,

Against all desire, I need you to balance the table at a dinner tomorrow evening here at Spencer House. Wear your emerald green dress. Do try to be less of the attitude I found you in this afternoon.

Your Aunt

Bother and a half.

August 18th

Agnes decided to wax philosophical while polishing the silver today.

She spoke for an hour straight. None of it worth the time to write down.

Later

Miss Hunt, Roland's current liability, was at Aunt Eugenia's dinner this evening. ~~I now refrain from making a snide expression~~. I am undoubtedly making a snide expression. Her hair was bound in a severe fashion. She tilted her head so that her diamond earrings would catch the light—it resulted in her looking like a bird. She wore orange and she deserved it.

Throughout the entire dinner, she endeavoured to laugh in the popular female way, i.e., as the tinkling of a merry bell.

She accomplished it.

It sounded less ghastly than I would have liked.

In sum, she vexed me.

When the ladies passed through, I sought refuge from the storm. A small settee near the window—too small for a comfortable duo of any size—was my raft of choice. I was Robinson Caruso. No, that's not right. Coruso…? Curso…? Crusoe! Ha! That's it. I was Robinson Crusoe, determined to survive. Or so I like to believe. I've never actually read the book. Does he survive? Does he return hideously scarred? Does he have a limp? And why? Also, why does The Tenant, a one Niall Pierce, whose first name usage has been unrevoked, have a limp? And would he tell me if I asked?

I digress.

There I was, happily looking out the window, when Miss Hunt appeared near me. She smiled expectantly. And I, ever the paragon of middling manners, did not trouble with a winning smile. Instead, I put forth a small, surprised one.

"Oh, hello," I said. The *oh* and the *hello* both said with the same tone.

Rude? No.

Discourteous? It could be argued.

Self-preservation? Most certainly.

"Miss Lion. We were at the far end of the table and have not yet had a chance to talk."

"Imagine," I answered.

She looked towards the settee expectantly.

It was a moment of decision.

My mother once told me she'd hope I'd live without guile.

"No, no, love," my father had answered from across the room, bent over one of his illustrations. "Let her keep just a wee bit. She'll need it. Not too much!" he added when he saw my mother's face.

Be it guile or not, there was a significant fight between my good nature and my everyday one. In the end they both turned against me, and I found myself sweetening my smile and arranging myself so the elegant and orange Miss Hunt could sit. It took both of us leaning away from one another to manage two sets of hips.

"I thought we would have met sooner than this!" Miss Hunt exclaimed. "My mother and your aunt have become friendly. I've seen hours of Arabella. We're very *simpatico!* (a thing I doubt). There have been some very select gatherings, the best society has to offer. Yet I haven't seen you at any of them!" She spoke the words with a smile, but there was a cunning in her eyes. One might even say that my little measure of guile is nothing compared to hers.

Mother, be proud.

"Hmm," I replied.

"What was that you said?" she asked, tilting her head, forcing more than a single syllable reply.

I honestly don't know what people want from other people. What have we come to if there is no room for a one-syllable reply? The exception being Islington, Duke of, saying *"Ah."* We all agree he is below board. "We all" being society in general, of whom I have decided to become representative in this matter. My newly self-appointed presidency of the Single Syllable Society, however, did not awe Miss Hunt. I don't believe she even acknowledged it had taken place.

Alas, it had to be done. An answer had to be given. "I have been in my aunt's company from time to time, but I am kept very busy with my own schedule, you see. But how charming for Arabella that you have become so close."

She smiled so as to wrinkle her nose.

(I raise a single eyebrow at the memory.)

"We will have to speak more when Mr. Sutherland fulfils his promised opera," I finished.

"Oh, haven't you heard?" Her eyes widened. She paused, her lips parted, the story on the tip of her *pointed* tongue. She could not conceal her pleasure.

Yet she did not speak, making me ask the abominable, "Heard what?"

"He broke his arm! Poor soul!" (Correction: Roland Sutherland is not poor, however injured he may be.) "He shattered it into a million pieces and has been abed in the country! I'd have thought you would have known! Your being such great friends and all. I'm surprised, truly!"

It was not a moment I was willing to turn the other cheek.

"Oh, Roland and I don't communicate such dull things," I replied. "If it's not a broken neck, Miss Hunt, I can't see any fuss."

I smiled.

She gave a diffused laugh.

Diffused laughter. Who has any use for it?

Muffled? Certainly.

Laughter cut short? Obviously.

Diffused? Aggravating.

Needless to say, I left said party at the earliest opportunity.

Ironically, what was waiting when I arrived home?

Emma,

I don't know if you are aware, but I have broken my arm to pieces. Lord Bennington's housekeeper has put me under lock and key. I didn't think the British Parliament granted her the authority for such a thing. As it is, I would love to see you once I'm able to jailbreak and return home to London, which should be within a day or two.

Roland

I shook my head and climbed upstairs to my garret, where I penned a response.

Roland,

You goat! Do you know who told me you had broken your arm? Miss Hunt. Miss Hunt! You foul, foul creature.

How are you feeling?

Emma

Having discharged that duty, I opened a second letter that proved to be a note, actually.

E,

Care to tell me what you were doing in the East End and who you were with?

J

Dear me.
J is for snake.
And Jack.

Where I was and who I was with is none of his business.
Now all I can think of is Everett's apple tartlets.

August 19th

Niall Pierce

EMMA LION?

I woke this morning quite convinced we two have filled the quota for All Serious Things.

Something must be done.

HAVE YOU A REMEDY TO SUGGEST?

Humour or distraction. I'm certain one or the other will alleviate our current state of woe.

WOE?

Woe, Pierce. We are in woe.

I'VE BEEN A GREAT MANY THINGS, MISS LION, BUT NEVER IN WOE.

How sad!

IS IT?

Perhaps it is even woeful.

PERHAPS YOU ARE MAD.

I thought you knew that already.

TEA AT THE REED AND RITE, THEN A PERUSAL OF THE KEEP? TOMORROW?

Pardon?

I'M SUGGESTING A REMEDY TO OUR JOINT WOE.

I thought you did not believe in woe.

MAD, I TELL YOU.

August 20th

—Animorum Impulsu et coeca magnaque cupidine ducti.

JUV. SAT. X. 350.

By blind impulse of eager passion driven.

The smile on my face can only be described as stupid. Or intoxicated. Or both.

But not from wine. Rather, Latin.

To be specific, a small black volume fat enough to promise happiness.

This morning went as well as could be expected. Dr. Fairchild came to check on Cousin Archibald. It was deemed necessary I be present. I did not deem. Neither did Archibald deem. However, Dr. Fairchild deemed, and so I stood sulkily in the corner while the prostrate figure in the bed sulkily wiped sweat from his face and spoke of the calculated abuses I had wrought upon his person. (A majority categorically untrue as Parian has served as intermediary for the last week and I have not had opportunity for any abuse, calculated or otherwise.) Speaking of Parian, he was there as well, standing sulkily beside the bed, waiting for Dr. Fairchild to finish his examination before providing his weasel-like frame as support should Fairchild order Archibald to his feet.

There was a significant amount of sulk to be shared by all.

After a thorough examination, Fairchild announced Cousin Archibald should wait until the beginning of next month, ten days, before beginning to walk with assistance.

The relief on Cousin Archibald's face was evident; however much he roundly berated Fairchild, myself, and Young Hawkes for the many injustices of his situation.

"Young Hawkes has nothing to do with your current state," I snapped from a safe vantage. (He can throw neither plate nor glass to the far corner, a hypothesis we in the scientific community of Lapis Lazuli House have had ample opportunity to test and confirm, giving this world a new, indelible fact.)

"Hawkes owes me a visit! I've complaints to make! I've not seen him in days and days!"

"His ministry extends beyond bitter old men."

"You—"

But it was never revealed what he was to say, for Fairchild cleared his throat and said he would return next week.

My productive morning included dusting the garret, the entire fourth floor, and the drawing room, followed by an hour at the window, and a small exchange with Mrs. Morrow yelled through the very same window, who said that Mr. Able's son had seen The Roman in Baron's Square near the fountain of Perseus and Medusa the night before last.

"Quite the cultured ghost," I remarked.

"Oh, I expect he just pretends to know what it's all about, like the rest of us," came her answer.

I'm suspect of the notion he hasn't learned his Greek mythology by now. What else has he to do?

Luncheon was had in the breakfast room, which Agnes thought was so amusing.

"It's the wrong time a day, ya ken?"

The Reed and Rite
For a Cup of Tea

Pierce and I, through wall negotiation, arranged a time to meet at the Reed and Rite.

Feeling better than I was when the outing had been arranged, I wore my bottle green afternoon dress with my red gloves, feeling like a garden.

When I walked in, I saw Pierce sitting in the corner near our window.

He was busy scribbling something and did not look up until I was three steps from the table. "Hello," he said as he stood, then moved towards my chair. But as I was already seeing to the job, I waved him off and we sat.

"Anything important?" I asked, indicating his scribbles.

"I've had some more requests for portraits. I'm gathering a loose version of my schedule so I might set the times."

Over tea—coffee for Pierce—he mentioned having unpacked a box and discovered an entire volume of Emerson's essays.

"I've another in my effects to be sent from America, so you are welcome to defile this copy with arguments to your contrary heart's content. If you're not afraid to take him on again."

"Your Mr. Emerson doesn't scare me," I answered. "Now that I've seen his back, I doubt he'll hold much sway."

He gave me a token smile.

"I've been thinking of that photograph you showed me, the one with Mr. Emerson."

Pierce waited for me to continue.

"There was a woman with the group," I added.

"Wise you are Emma, for it is the woman in white whom you should fear."

Niall Pierce rose in my estimation.

I enjoy a man who can unironically speak of fearing women.

"Who is she?"

Pierce leaned against the corner so that his shoulders were offset towards the rest of the room and looked past me. "That photograph is the only I've ever taken of her, on the single occasion I was able to convince her to leave her house in my company."

"A recluse?"

"Yes. And no. Her soul isn't bound by four walls."

"I'm intrigued. Are you intimate friends?"

"No. That is to say, I suppose. In our way. We've written a good deal the last ten years. She's—well, she's not afraid of what I do, and I'm not afraid of what she does."

"Heavens. What does she do?"

Then he tilted his head dismissively. "She keeps her secrets." And he left it at that.

The Keep
For a Missing Pen Knife with the Unbelieving

A perusal of The Keep revealed a pillow belonging to the Lapis Lazuli drawing room (I'd wondered where it had been misplaced), and Pierce found a pen knife with his initials on it that he didn't even realise he was missing.

"Jolly you found it!" I called from behind a pile of unfinished embroideries—rarely claimed.

"It's bloody impossible," he answered, his veiled agitation not so veiled.

The Dalliance
Books of the New, Slightly Used, & Abominably Treated Yet Resurrected Variety

As we walked up Whereabouts towards home, we noticed an unusual number of people inside The Dalliance. Three more steps brought us in view of the placard in the window.

"Ah! It's a raffle!" I cried in triumph.

Pierce frowned. "Is this another of your absurd traditions?"

"Not absurd at all!" I answered. And ordering he follow me, we crowded in, claiming the wall to the right of the door.

Mr. Graves, bookseller and critic of Emma M. Lion, was helping customers and handing out tickets.

"What sort of raffle is this?" Pierce asked, his deep voice almost lost beneath the chatter of the scene.

"A few times every year, Mr. Graves holds a raffle. He gives a ticket for each book purchased, and then the winning ticket gets *that.*" I pointed to a book wrapped in decorative paper, sitting atop a table display.

"That's all?"

"What do you mean 'that's all'?" It was my expression, rather than my words, that quelled Pierce into silent acceptance that the beauty was in the simplicity. He left me against the wall and began to wander, picking up this and that odd volume until he found something that caught enough of his attention to merit the turning of several pages.

Without more reference than his cursory glance—unaware that several customers of the female variety were giving him a cursory glance for their reference—he went to the counter and purchased his book. Mr. Graves wrapped the book in paper and handed Pierce a ticket.

The crowd had grown, and so it took a little maneuvering for him to return to our place against the wall.

"You found something to catch your attention?" I asked, eyeing the book with more than a little envy.

"I did."

And he did not say anything more!

No title! No hint!

It felt like an excessive amount of privacy to me, but I held my tongue and was rewarded for it. For he handed me his ticket.

"This is for you. Best of luck."

"Pierce! How lovely of you!"

Only a few moments later, Mr. Graves called the crowd to order, made a speech about the need to support the written word (hear, hear!) and the need to buy more books from The Dalliance rather than other bookshops about London, his establishment being "far superior to your run-of-the-mill shop" one finds about *These Days*.

These Days?

(I'm someday going to write an entire volume on everything These Days.)

Mr. Graves asked a young man to play a rousing march—on a trumpet of all things—before drawing the winning number.

A glance around the shop revealed dozens of hopeful faces.

Pierce excepting. He was unsmiling but amused at our expense, I'm certain of it.

I held the red ticket in my red gloves, willing myself to be the victor.

Graves, deciding he'd had enough of suspense, rattled off the number.

"53!"

And I couldn't believe it. For the ticket in my hand was printed with a handsome *53*.

"I won!" I shouted, and everybody turned and murmured. The tide of people practically shoved me to where Mr. Graves stood, utterly displeased with what fate had delivered.

I produced my ticket, had a small argument regarding the legality of my win as I had not purchased the book, and then Pierce came to my defence, looking rather tall as he stated that he and I had gone in on the book together, and yes, we also shared the ticket. Thank you.

Reluctantly, Graves handed it over, and the crowd gave a token cheer as they began to disperse.

I did not unwrap my prize immediately. Once we were out on the street, I held it up triumphantly and asked Pierce, "Are you prepared for the glory of this moment?"

"Fire away," he replied, his own book tucked beneath his arm.

I tore the paper off, revealing a pleasantly sized black book. When I turned it over, the title caused Pierce to laugh outright.

Latin Phrases for the Unrepentant

It was the most beautiful thing I had ever seen.

"Wonderful!" I exclaimed, and those waiting to see the prize agreed.

As we walked home—I thumbing through and repeating phrases aloud—Pierce's mouth maintained an upward tick, however slightly. "Only you would win such a book," he muttered.

To which I replied, *"Fata viam invenient."*

August 21st

This morning I was paid a call. An Illustrious one to boot.

I was upstairs with *Latin Phrases for the Unrepentant* when Agnes braved the journey. "You've a caller, Miss Lion. I've put him in the drawing room. And offered him tea. And cake. And sticky toffee pudding."

Her cheeks were pink. Her eyes alight. She shone with the joy of ten thousand suns. It was certainly damning evidence pointing towards a certain duke.

"I'll be right down, Agnes. Don't hover."

I first approached the drawing room by means of stealth—an alternative way to say I hunched down and peered through the keyhole. Emma M. Lion, adult extraordinaire.

Islington was settled in the far corner of the green sofa. Legs crossed, elbow on the arm of the sofa, hand lifted to the side of his face. His ducal gaze was absently focused on the pink chair before him.

It is without dispute. The men of my acquaintance have commandeered my green sofa with admirable ease.

Straightening myself, I entered and offered what I thought to be a perfectly reasonable greeting. "Islington. You are a glutton for punishment."

He glanced my way, stood, offered a silent yet polite bow, and settled when I did, regaining his position of controlled comfort.

"Miss Lion. I trust you are well this morning?"

"I am well. And you?"

"The same, thank you."

"Agnes tells me she's already offered you tea. And cake. And sticky toffee pudding! I hope you weren't overwhelmed."

His hazel eyes glanced from me to the door. "You've a very generous household. Please take no offence that I declined the sticky toffee."

"Am I to assume then that you accepted the cake?"

With a slow blink and that very put together look of his, Islington replied, "Who would not want cake?"

As if on cue, Agnes arrived with some antiquated tea trolley she must have found in a forgotten corner of Lapis Lazuli House. It was clean but squeaked something terrible. I applaud Islington for keeping a straight face, for I could not.

"Oh dear, Agnes. Where did you find that dragon?"

Agnes, giving the racket no mind, watched the duke with—and I lie not—veiled eyes. "Only the best, Miss Lion."

I. Lie. Not.

Only the best.

What was the girl thinking?

His Grace gave a perfunctory smile that lasted for the two seconds Agnes dared look at his face. She fussed over the tea. Too long. My wish was to spare her. "Do let me, Agnes. Yes, leave the tea trolley here. It looks lovely. Yes. Quite. Thank you, Agnes. It is the finest tea this house has seen."

"Thank you, Miss," she said breathlessly.

After a rather deep bow, she left. I felt cruel, separating her from the object of her newfound affection.

"You have a devotee, Duke," I remarked after she left.

He said nothing, and I prepared two cups of tea and cut two slices of a lovely sponge cake.

We ate in relative silence. I believe we were weighing one another. Taking stock.

Admittedly, he gained a point in my esteem for the way he pressed his fork against the crumbs left on his plate, controlled yet absent at the same time. When he spoke, it was not what I was expecting.

"How's your friend Mr. Hollingstell?" asked Islington.

I began to prepare us each a second cup of tea. "I have no idea. I haven't seen him in almost a month. Why do you ask?"

The duke cleared his throat. "Because I saw him the other night."

I did not mean to look so surprised. "Where could you possibly have seen him?"

"At the opera. When I was alone, he slipped into my box."

"But that's against my rules," I blurted out. Foolishly.

"Ah," he answered. Like he had caught me out.

Ah.

Maddening, maddening man.

Looking very directly at me, he continued, "Hollingstell indicated that you were willing to play with fire on *my* account. That he was to leave me be. He wanted to know why." Pause, and then, "As do I."

"Oh, Jack, you fool," I muttered. Then, "You, Islington, were *not* singled out. There was an agreement. Having come inside the sphere of my world, you benefit from said agreement, as do my other associates. You are not special."

"A relief to know."

I blanched. "I didn't mean it in *that* way. Certainly, to someone you are the most special person in all the world. I meant that I made a deal with Jack—Mr. Hollingstell—because he is a villainous snake, however much he enjoys feeding me pastries."

The duke checked at the mention of the pastries.

I suppose I should have clarified that Jack has never *fed* me hand to mouth.

Islington did not seek said clarification and instead asked, "What deal have you made?"

"That is my own affair."

"Clearly it's not," he retorted. "I am now party. This snake of yours found his way into my opera box."

"You are not party," I argued. "I am party. You are the blissful ignorant. Jack was simply creeping about. I shall take him to task for it."

He laughed then. His honed, practiced laugh.

"I do not need *you* to protect me from anyone," he stated, as if it were law.

"Agreed! With the exception of Jack. It was done wholesale, Islington. The agreement included all of my acquaintances. Jack would leave my people in peace, and I would— Well, an arrangement was made. Had it happened a month sooner, it would not have included you. He would have been free to fleece you for every pound you possess. Alas, fate seems to have it out for me. There is no escaping cosmic humour in Lapis Lazuli House."

I spread my hands out to add veracity to my claim.

He tilted his head slightly, a hard, disbelieving smile on his face. Then he said, and I quote, "Either a friendship with you is the grandest thing in the world, Miss Lion, or you are delusional. Which is it?"

An unfair question, I felt.

Surely there is room for a degree of both?

"I defer to your wisdom to sort that out, Islington."

He gave a half laugh and then stood.

I followed suit.

Agnes had left his hat and gloves on the round table, so I brought them to him. As he was putting them on, he said, "Please keep me out of all future—*ah*, how would one say it?—Gutter Street arrangements?"

I resisted making a face. Only Just. "I will try."

"As you have chivalrously taken it upon yourself to protect me from the threat that is Mr. Jack Hollingstell—certainly not his real name—keep your sword sharp. Also"—and beneath his ducal polish there was some brand of sincerity—"come and see me if you need help. Strictly as a humble squire to your glorified knighthood. I do not repeat the mistake of implying you are incapable."

And before Agnes could make her way from the kitchen, he was across the hall and out the door.

"Has he gone, Miss?"

"He has, Agnes."

She sighed.

I did not.

August 22nd

A day of dubious luck concerning the post.

Why dubious?

The definition of the word 'dubious' carries a degree of the suspect. It is a grand fit for the occasions of ~~life~~ my life. One might write an ode.

Ode to the Dubious Life of Emma M. Lion

Now I'm recalling Milton's 'dubious battle' and wondering what Cousin Archibald did with that copy of *Paradise Lost* I was reading in March… Speaking of dubious things.

My first piece of mail is on the more promising side of suspect.

For I, Emma M. Lion, received an invitation that was not of my aunt's contrivance.

Wonders never cease.

As it happens, the Lady Trewartha of Baron's Square throws an exclusive soiree at the end of each August to say farewell to the Season. I have been sent an invitation due to my St. Crispian's residency.

It is prestigious.

I know for fact that Cousin Archibald has never been invited.

It is to be held on the thirty-first. The invitation card—a deep blue embossed with gold—stated after the pertinent details, "When the boring have fled London, let us make merry."

I am intrigued. And more than a little pleased.

I've no idea how my invitation came about.

The second piece of post is suspect by association, as it's from dear Aunt Eugenia.

Emma,

Tomorrow is the Duchess of Bedford's ball. Arrive at my house no later than four o'clock. We will have tea, fit your gown, and while Arabella rests, the maids will see what they can do with your general appearance.

This is the final event of The Season. You are to help lure the gentlemen on the enclosed list into at least two Gazes and one Conversation.

Do not disappoint me.

I read it aloud to Tybalt, who looked at me for almost a minute and then blinked slowly in agreement with Aunt Eugenia.

It wasn't the show of loyalty I was hoping for.

August 23rd

The Duchess of Bedford's ball was an absolute ten to one lark.

Let the record show I enjoyed myself immensely.

I laughed more than I have in… Goodness, I've no idea.

Were Oliver and Phineas Brookstone ever in finer form? I think not.

As for my own triumph, Charles Goddard failed miserably to secure a dance, however persistently he followed me about the floor.

And Islington! How deftly he handled the entire affair…

I see I'm getting ahead of myself.

Journals are meant to be chronological affairs, as proven not only by my own but that of the estimable Islington. I will endeavour to hold the course.

It all began when I took a hansom cab to Aunt Eugenia's—blessed indulgence, for her footmen always pay the driver.

Upon arrival, I was ushered into Arabella's room.

"There you are," Arabella said from her chaise lounge. "Mother was quite despairing we would have any time to make you presentable after tea."

I took off my red gloves and laid them on Arabella's bed. "I don't have to look presentable. I only have to keep Phineas and Oliver Brookstone from proposing to you."

"You will look presentable. You will say little to nothing. You will follow every order," came the command as Aunt Eugenia entered. "I expected you an hour ago. Now, change into the dress you see there"—she pointed towards a shimmering, champagne-coloured ball gown, far beyond my social currency—"and do nothing else until the maid has rectified your entire person." She then frowned, the line of her double chin expressing identical displeasure. "I turn my attention from you for two days, and look how unprepossessing you look! Does your chaperone not keep you from looking like a flower girl in the market? I can see I shall have to keep a closer eye."

My eyes grew wide at the mention of my chaperone, who is kind enough to be nonexistent.

"Mama," Arabella redirected, "I was hoping I could wear your blue diamonds tonight."

"Blue? No, no. Blue is for next Season. Blue diamonds make even the men salivate. You will wear my teardrop diamonds, and that will be the end of it. Now, Emma, do try and pull yourself together. The Duchess of Bedford has an ugly daughter, and we must not distract anyone from that fact."

"I won't let you down, Aunt," I answered as Arabella tilted her head in lazy amusement, her golden curls arranged to perfection.

Tea was had.

Aunt Eugenia left the room just as the maid entered.

"Your mother thinks my hair too wild," I said.

"I think it lovely, Emma," Arabella sighed. "It will tell any man what he's in for."

The maid began helping me from my clothes and into the ball gown.

"I've no intention of telling a man anything, Arabella," I said.

"Nonsense. Of course you will be matched in this life. You need such a thing, I believe."

"Do I?" I challenged. "And do you recommend I use your strategy? Whatever man has the most money, the greatest number of houses, and least number of attractive features?"

"Oh no," Arabella waved. "You marry a handsome man with a pleasing face. Then we can both enjoy looking at him. Leave the money to me."

I grunted suspiciously.

The gown fit like perfection. I've never worn anything that shimmered to such a degree, and I admit to liking it very much. Bless Phineas and Oliver Brookstone. Perhaps I will use them in the future to augment my entire wardrobe.

The candleli—

!!!

A spider just dropped onto the page! Goodness. My entire spine shivered up and down. I slammed my journal shut—of course—and then had to fetch a handkerchief to wipe the remains away. As luck would have it, the spider met his demise on the words of Aunt Eugenia.

Fitting.

I digress.

The candlelight of Arabella's room made me look almost fetching—having my hair styled by her Parisian maid did contribute a certain *je ne sais quoi* to the ensemble.

Even Aunt Eugenia sniffed in a not disapproving way.

While Arabella rested, I was put through three hours of vigorous training regarding the men whose attention I was to direct towards Arabella.

It very nearly did me in.

Once Arabella was woken, all attendance was danced upon her until she shimmered with perfection. Then finally we were off.

All prior experience or expectation of what a ball ought to be was soundly thrashed. The Belgravia House? Devastating in its beauty. I walked through the incandescent rooms knowing that the value of everything in my bank accounts could not have paid for the candles, let alone the crystal, the flowers, the music. The gentlemen's suits. The gowns…

It was everything in first order.

It did not take long for me to ~~find the~~ hunt down the Brookstone twins and threaten them that if they did not let me enjoy the evening, I would personally put snakes in their beds.

"Hold on, mad thing," smiled Oliver. "We won't make you waste your evening on our trail, but it couldn't hurt for your aunt to believe we're a handful."

"Let your aunt think you're keeping us at bay. Really, you'll be free to do whatever you like," echoed Phineas. "We won't fail you, Emma."

And they didn't.

Phineas and Oliver Brookstone are the most comical souls I know, so sharp in their observations I found it unsafe to drink anything within earshot of their banter. I'd heard it was possible to laugh so hard one's drink would enter one's nose.

Well, I've now proven the theory.

The twins performed, approaching Arabella's exalted direction whenever Aunt Eugenia glared their way—her eyes bulged each attempt—and all I had to do was place my hands on their arms and make a show of distracting them. It was smoothly done. I even danced with each of them. Twice.

As for the holy task set before me, the Listed Gentlemen—nine in total—were easy to direct. Everyone stared at Arabella the night through as it was, and I had no difficulty ensuring their repeated attentions. Mr. George West took more effort; he kept getting turned around, dazzled not by the lights but by the moths flapping about them. It was only by noting that the shimmering pink of Arabella's gown was so like a sweet pea I had once seen in Bournemouth that I was able to direct his attention. That is, only after he had asked for the exact address and withdrew from his pocket a notebook.

I rattled off the first address I could think of in the miserable place—and afterward hid myself in a corridor, laughing at the thought of him trespassing in Cousin Matilde's garden. They would terrify one another.

At some point in the evening, Aunt Eugenia accused me of being in High Joviality, a thing unacceptable in my role as Foil to Arabella.

"I am foil, Aunt! Arabella is the heroine and I the comic fool," I said, grinning after she had caught me crying with laughter at something Oliver had said about the Marchioness of Gainsbourg.

"I want you to be the poor, pitiable foil, Emma. Cease looking so pleased with yourself immediately!"

Sigh.

After a number of hours and a dozen dances, as I was watching the general glittering exhibition, I found a duke at my elbow.

I suppose such things happen in Belgravia.

"Miss Lion."

"Islington."

He looked as well put together as any of the men there—not a little achievement—shoulders straight to the point of stiffness, not a hair out of place, his hazel eyes in the maddening, middling place between engagement and disengagement. His tone of voice mimicked his appearance when he said, "May I express some surprise at seeing you at the Duchess of Bedford's ball? You do not strike me as one of her usual guests."

It was mildly insulting. He *could* have led with, "How your gown shimmers."

Alas.

Fortunate for him I was in high humour.

When I opened my mouth to say something clever, he added, "Her guests usually lack a certain verve which you seem to carry in abundance, is all."

"Is that supposed to be a compliment?"

"Certainly." The duke's accompanying smile was controlled. "Many of her acquaintances are political."

"Political, meaning…?"

"Stuffy. Boring. Angling." He looked around the glimmering room. "Have you seen the library?"

"No."

"You should sometime. Care to dance?"

It was a confusing misdirection. The promise of a Belgravia library only to be swept away by an invitation to dance. It was at this exact moment I felt the adoring gaze of Charles Goddard from across the room. There had been tremendous effort put into the avoidance of the man, and I wasn't going to let it all go to waste.

"Now look at what you've done, Islington."

"What's that?"

"Charles Goddard. That giraffe making his way towards us. My unintended Intended, if I am correct."

Islington's veneer broke to acknowledge some confusion on his part. "*That* man is your intended?"

"Certainly not," I rejoined. "I said he was my *unintended* Intended. I never said they were *my* intentions. My aunt, after another Season of humble servitude to her Machiavellian plans, would happily see me married off to him so that I might produce tall babies."

"The threats you battle are real, Miss Lion."

"Every day a test of my very survival. Oh dear. He's made it through that scrum of dowagers. There's no stopping him now. Brace yourself for uninspiring conversation with a waistcoat."

Islington, I must admit, is nothing if not grace under fire. He did not bat an eye. Before Charles Goddard could get close enough to make any claim on my attention, Islington took my elbow and we stepped out into the waltz.

"Well done," I stated, wide-eyed at the heroic intervention.

"I've managed my fair number of unintended Intendeds, Miss Lion."

Had he indeed? I tilted my head. "And here I was thinking your talents were to be found in your writing and general intimidation."

Islington, leading with admirable confidence, gave the flicker of an inside smile. "Speaking of, you will be happy to know that I've invested in a white feather, which I have placed over my current journal. All others have been removed to Stonecrop."

"Stonecrop?"

"My country seat."

"How very aristocratic of you. *My* country seat is in the back garden of Lapis Lazuli."

His expression closed a little.

I shouldn't have said it, I suppose. It was meant only as a bit of humour.

After a moment I said, "It's lovely."

"Pardon?"

"The name. Stonecrop. Where is it?"

"Derbyshire."

It was, perhaps, too much to ask I refrain from any literary references. I tried, but my expression froze on the rather mischievous end, and he gave me a put-upon expression. "Go ahead. Make your jest."

"Is it in the miserable half?" I blurted joyfully.

"No," he almost snapped.

"I take it you've heard that before."

Islington pulled me closer to him as we spun—it was very prettily done, and all to his credit, for I'm an adequate dancer at most—and said, "I'm surprised they allowed you to read such outmoded fiction at Fortitude, A Preparatory School for Girls."

"Contraband."

"*Ah.*"

I laughed.

Then, out of the corner of my eye, I saw something rather great and terrible.

"Oh dear. Now look what you've done, Islington."

"You've said that twice now. Is that unfortunate young man still on our trail?"

"Worse. Look over my shoulder. Do you see that formidable gathering of society matrons just there? The one in the silver beaded dress is my aunt. If she were to see us dancing, doom would descend."

"Doom?"

"Doom. She belongs to the first order of gorgons."

He looked towards Aunt Eugenia as if he weren't afraid. It was too cavalier, especially as how that was the exact moment my aunt gave a cursory glance across the dance floor. "Careful," I hissed. "She will turn you to stone."

"I've managed my fair number of gorgons, Miss Lion."

"Have you? What a regular Perseus you are," I snapped as he *deftly* moved us towards the opposite side of the dance floor.

"Perseus did not turn the Gorgon to stone on his own merit. He had help from Athena," he replied.

"Did he? Point for you, Islington; I did not know that."

"Owing to your faulty education?" he said in a cheeky tone.

"Yes, actually. All heathenistic myths were banned. But I know all of the Beatitudes."

"Blessed are the meek," he answered dryly. "How then did you discover Perseus?"

"My father."

And Islington stopped. It took me a moment to realise the music had as well.

His arms loosened unexpectedly, and I almost stumbled backward.

The waltz was over.

"Your aunt is making her way towards us," he remarked calmly.

He was right. There was Aunt Eugenia, arms swinging, diamonds sparkling, willing herself to go faster. Fortunately, his back was to her so she could not see his face.

"Go now, Islington. She *will* turn you to stone. And then eat you."

"I'm not intimidated."

"How very naive. You must not know my aunt."

"Lady Spencer, I believe. And while I am not intimidated by wealthy women with beautiful daughters, I do tend to avoid them. Goodnight, Miss Lion."

After dancing so closely together, I thought he would be gallant and kiss my glove.

He did not.

Rather, he seemingly took pleasure at delivering me to my doom. Then, with a subtle tilt of the head, he stepped into the masses. By the time Aunt Eugenia reached my side, the Duke of Islington was no more than a dream.

I will confess this much, the man certainly knows how to waltz.

"Emma!" Aunt Eugenia hissed when she arrived at my side. "What in heaven's name do you think you are doing?"

"I was dancing, Aunt."

"I saw that. With whom?"

Athena, being the Goddess of Wisdom, thought it wise to keep Perseus's name and rank out of the gorgon's reach.

"An acquaintance, is all."

"You are not to be dancing with a man who looks like that, Emma."

"Did you see his face?"

"No, not clearly. But there was certainly a sense of good breeding and general appeal about his person. Mediocrity, that's what I expect from you until Arabella is married."

"And then?"
"Plebeian Respectability."
How enlightening, Aunt. My future life sounds a triumph.
It was then that the Brookstones made a direct line towards Arabella and I was dispatched to head them off at the pass.
There turned out to be no time to go in search of the library, but, all in all, I rather enjoyed myself.

My one and a half windows are open, and I think I just now heard the sound of the front door swinging. It does need to be oiled.
I shall go down and investigate before changing out of my gown.
Perhaps Parian didn't close it all the way. His laziness is almost monumental.

Later

I just had the most surreal experience.
I am not sure what to make of it.
It felt…
Well, it felt like one of Father's fairy tales.
My skirt gathered in one hand, I made my way quietly down the stairs in my bare feet, without the light of a candle. When I reached the hall, the front door was swinging open like it had been forgotten. Instead of closing it, I stood there awhile in the warm night, the air sweeter than I recalled it being when I arrived home an hour before.
And so, being a good Irishman's daughter, I went out.
It was still on the street. Not a soul on Whereabouts Lane. There was light from the streetlamps, but all the windows were dark. I half expected to see The Roman. A breeze threaded its way through the back gardens of Whereabouts, and a few errant summer leaves were blown into a whirl down the lane.
And then I saw a figure walking up from King Henry's Road. A dark form at first, it was not until I recognised the limp that I knew it to be Pierce.
He moved through the circles cast down by the streetlamps, a

jacket over one shoulder. And it was not until he was twenty paces away that he looked up and saw me.

He did not say anything. He simply stopped and considered for a full minute before continuing to walk slowly towards me. It was too sensory—if that is the right word—the sound of his footsteps on the sidewalk, the sweet tang of an air not usually found in London, the press of the pavement against my bare feet. As he came closer, walking in a half circle around me, his eyes missing nothing, all thoughts of dancing and the twins and Arabella and Islington evaporated.

In the entirety of my life, I do not believe I have ever been looked at in such a way. It was all encompassing, honest, and reverent somehow. He smelled rather wonderful, and I moved my hand, only just, so as to touch him, as if I doubted he was flesh and blood.

I'm sounding ridiculous, but it was so very strange.

Then he stopped, our shoulders shy of touching.

"What witchery are you up to on a night such as this?"

It was a moment for Shakespeare. Or Wordsworth.

Any poetry, really.

And all I could think of to say was, "I was closing a door."

He tilted his head and half a smile came with it. "But fey doors never quite close, do they?"

And for a moment I… I almost… It wasn't intentional or thought out. Only, looking up at him, I almost wondered if he would…

And then the monks began to sing.

The monks. At Jacob's Well.

Gregorian chants in harmony with the breeze.

We both glanced up the lane towards the sound. Whatever spell there was did not break. Rather, it shifted. He turned. And we were standing side by side, watching the darkness.

I shivered, although not with cold, yet he took his jacket and dropped it over my shoulders, the scent of storm and musk coming with it.

We did not speak for a quarter of an hour.

Then, "It's late."

That was all he said. He looked down at me once more, his face at home in the shadows, and stepped away. A moment later he was through his door, and I was alone again on the street.

August 24th

I woke disoriented just now. My tired mind filled with the stuff dreams are made of. (Ah, Shakespeare, you have all the words.) Glancing around the garret, I took note of yesterday's spoils. There were my shoes toppled on the floor, the beautiful gown I'd managed to pull myself from with the help of a crochet hook, my reticule. My muddled thoughts were filled with images of my aunt, the Brookstone twins, Islington.

And Niall Pierce's jacket folded atop the bookshelf.

It provided an instantaneous resurrection. I was wide awake.

Mortified.

Had I really believed I would…?

I reread last night's entry.

Ridiculous.

How silly. I wouldn't have wanted to, anyway.

It was simply a witching hour.

I was most certainly not going to kiss Niall Pierce. I've never even ~~thought of it before~~ thought of it very seriously before. What a load of rubbish—and a relief I did not let myself get carried away.

I am his landlady. He is my tenant.

Friendship and first names not excepting.

I'm certain there are Laws against such things.

If not, Rules, at the very least.

Also, as Agnes pointed out not too many days past, I know nothing of him save the following: He is a photographer of war. He lived in New York. He has strange friends. He limps. He does not care for the British government. He enjoys a well-put-together room. And he occupies space differently than anyone I know.

Yes, Mr. Pierce, I grant that you are notable.

But to think of anything else is absurd.

Plebeian Respectability. That is what we are striving for.

As a show of good faith towards such goals, I intend to take his jacket down to him this morning with occupied indifference.

Later

After readying myself in the mirror—doing my hair plainly for a less enchanted encounter—I took the jacket downstairs and was equal parts relief and dread when I heard Pierce working about his studio.

I knocked.

He answered, "Come in."

I opened the door and stepped inside.

It turns out I needn't have worried last evening would have any effect on him.

Standing at the far end of the room, sorting through a stack of papers on the credenza, he passed his eyes over me in a very professional and impersonal manner. "Good morning."

Then he was back to sorting his papers.

"Good morning." I lifted the arm I'd folded his jacket over. "I've come to return this to you."

Not so much as a second glance. Only, "Ah, yes. Thank you. Would you mind terribly placing it over the sofa?"

Well.

Perhaps he'd had a little more to drink last night than I thought, for no recollection of our midnight encounter was apparent.

I laid his jacket down, smiling like a pleasant fool, in case he bothered to look.

He didn't.

And after a "Good day, Pierce," I left the salon.

Only, as soon as I turned my back, the sound of him rustling through his papers stopped, and I am almost certain I could feel him watching.

Most likely embarrassed for me.

And what I dislike most of all, aside from my own mortification, is the panicked feeling that Maxwell would… It's foolish, I know. But I can't help if he follows me about. And what if I were to want…? What if I only thought I did, but could only think of Maxwell? Could only *imagine* Maxwell.

Oh dear. Emma, pull yourself together!
It is time to redouble my efforts.
Latin, Emerson, and nothing more.

Later

Yesterday was the twenty-third.
I forgot to light a candle for Father.

August 25th

I've just finished scrubbing the west garret. Unable to sleep past dawn, I decided some dusting and arranging would do me and the garret some good. Tybalt stalked about, perching on the odd this or that, watching my progress like a factory foreman. (Not that I know a good deal about factories but for those dreadful romances that peppered the back channel reading of Fortitude, A Preparatory School for Girls.)

Glancing at myself in the mirror, I look like a charwoman, my hair bound up with an old bit of cloth, my worn dress in need of a wash, my face with a smudge of dirt.

Here is Parian coming up the stairs.

I can hear judgement in every step.

Later

Parian came to tell me that as Agnes was frolicking about London (I believe she went to the butcher's), it was his task to tell me that *he* wanted me.

He.

"He?" I enquired. "Cousin Archibald?" It was only half past nine in the morning, and I'd not thought he was even awake.

"No," Parian sniffed. "The other He."

And he left. He, Parian. Not He, The Other.

Well, Pierce may have seen me at my most enchanting, but as he's also seen me cry, I've no complaint of my appearance. *He* will just have to bear it out. As will I.

Later

Oh dear.

Dear me.

Blast.

He is *not* Pierce.

I am now scrambling about, washing my face, pinning my hair, and trying to remember that if I send Parian to the curb, I shall have to deal with Cousin Archibald myself.

Later

I have just spent the last hour walking about the park with Islington, Duke of.

It was not intended.

For the He who presented himself at Lapis Lazuli was none other than Roland Sutherland, injured sun god.

When I walked into the drawing room, brushing my hands against my skirt, I did not expect to be met with human perfection standing before the fireplace, hat in hand, broken arm in a sling.

"Emma Lion? Is that you? You're absolutely filthy."

I could either admit to the shame of my appearance or bear it out with stubborn dignity.

I chose the latter.

"You've seen me covered in mud, Roland. A little dirt should be of no surprise. Great things are coming to pass which require some work on my end."

"Yes, but"—and he smiled widely—"when one is five, mud is expected."

"Yes, as is having one's arm in a sling. Look at you."

It made him appear some sort of hero. He said smugly, "How else am I to attract the ladies?"

"Oh, you've no fear of that," I retorted. "Now, why have you come. Tea?"

"Walk about the park, actually, before the afternoon gets too warm. I expected you to be presentable enough to join me."

"I may never be presentable enough to be seen in your grand company. However," I answered with a bow, "give me ten minutes to try."

Calling Agnes to follow, I went upstairs, stripped off my filthy dress, washed myself as best I could with the water from the basin, pinned my hair from wild to wayward, and, with the help of Agnes, put on one of my afternoon dresses and a hat.

Before I knew what was happening, Agnes pinched both of my cheeks.

"Agnes!" I shouted. "Why would you do a thing like that!"

"I only thought to add some colour. My mother says—"

"Your mother is very wrong if she gave you such advice. Now, away with you. And never do that again."

She scurried down the stairs, and I glanced at the mirror to assess the damage. To say that my colour looked improved is beside the point.

The real event happened only a few moments into our stroll. I was telling Roland how I had passed the last month of summer when a tumble of boys, young men really, came screaming in some game. The glares of dowagers and gentlemen ~~couldn't stop them~~ be damned. I thought it good fun and games until they rushed past and one, losing his footing, tumbled directly into Roland's broken arm!

Roland spun away from the pain only to be hit again and almost knocked over. Catching himself with his right hand, Roland gained steady footing, and from the clench of his jaw and the impressive streak of curse words he did his utmost to curtail—a shame, for I was learning some new ones—it was clear he was in significant pain.

The boys ran as fast as they could.

Before I could step forward to help Roland stand upright, someone else did.

"Steady, Sutherland."

And there was Islington.

He was looking cool as he held onto Roland's elbow, assessing the pain in Roland's face with his hazel eyes. "Does it hurt a great deal?"

Roland began to shake his head, and so I said, "Of course it does. Look how pale he is."

That was when Islington realised it was Emma M. Lion standing in judgement.

He made a strange sound, a sort of sound coming through his closed mouth as if to say, "Of course Emma M. Lion would be found at the scene of the crime."

"Miss Lion."

"Islington."

"Were you the one to push him down?"

I glared and he turned his attention back to Roland.

"It's nothing," Roland tried to say.

"How fresh is that break? You should see a doctor, man. Where is your carriage?"

"I walked. Emma and I are… It's nothing, truly. I just need to catch my breath."

It was an exhibition of male ~~stubbornness~~ stupidity at its finest.

Apparently, Islington thought so as well.

"Look there. Lord Crane and his wife in their carriage." And then Islington did the unexpected—he called out in public. "Hello! Crane! Hello there."

Roland, grimacing, manfully tried not to grasp his broken arm. We watched as Islington approached the slowed carriage and motioned towards Roland.

"He needn't have done it," Roland said, his words tight. "But he's a dashed splendid fellow"—sharp intake of breath—"when playing cards."

At which point our dashed splendid fellow was waving us over.

The situation was sorted rather handsomely. Lord Crane and Roland attend the same club, apparently, and Crane was very willing to help. It was agreed that they would take Roland home and call the doctor.

"First, we must see Miss Lion home," Roland insisted.

"Oh no, Roland. Lady Crane will see you taken care of, and I shall be fine. We can speak tomorrow."

Lord Crane is not handsome.

Roland is divine.

Lady Crane did not look burdened at coming to Roland's rescue.

"But Emma—"

"Come, Sutherland. I'll see Miss Lion home. You attend to that arm," Islington insisted.

And with that, Roland was swept away from me, looking back, lifting his good hand in parting—rather like the heroine in a desperate romance, while the hero must stand and watch his true love driving away.

I made an amused sound at the thought, and Islington gave me a side-eye but said nothing.

"Back to Lapis Lazuli House, Miss Lion?" he said, fussing with his gloves.

"Oh no, I've just arrived," I answered. "You go. Not to Lapis Lazuli House, I mean. To wherever you came from. I mean to enjoy myself. It's still cool enough to be redeemable."

But instead of leaving, Islington nodded obligingly and fell into step.

And so we walked. There wasn't an abundance of conversation, and Islington seemed satisfied with such an arrangement. He did ask after Cousin Archibald, to which I replied, "He's still abed, but I expect he will be walking with a cane soon."

"And it is a coincidence that he has a broken leg and Sutherland, also in your company, has a broken arm?"

This man has amazing ideas as to my powers.

"What are you implying, Islington?"

"Nothing, other than noting that those close to you find themselves in, *ah*, straits."

"Straits?"

"Yes, straits leading to questionable passage."

"*Ah*," I said in return.

He sensed, in my tone of imitation, some mockery.

He was correct.

August 26th

I ordered Arabella to send round a fruit basket to Roland, with both our names on the card. She reported back that Roland has been put under lock and key by his valet.

Poor Roland.

August 28th

A letter from Miss March,

Dear Emma,

I am coming home. There is a limit to the number of Italian counts one can abide in any given season.

I expect to be in St. Crispian's before September is out, and look forward to seeing you.

Saff. March

How lovely!

August 30th

When I arrived home today, Niall Pierce was sitting on the front steps of Lapis Lazuli House, reading a copy of the Morning Post. He was informality personified, leaning with one elbow back, his legs stretched out with each foot on a different step. I was going to ask why he chose my steps rather than his own for an afternoon sit, but guessed it was for comfort. Whomever Cousin Archibald hired to install the front steps of Lapis Lazuli Minor had made a somewhat crooked job of it.

Our side of the street was in pleasant shadow, so when he motioned for me to join him, I did.

He straightened himself as I sat next to him.

"There was a volcano that erupted," he said without ceremony.

"Where?"

"The Sunda Strait. Krakatoa is what it's called. It happened three days ago."

"How horrible," I answered. And I began to read over his shoulder as if it were the most normal thing in the world. One particular line caught my attention, and I repeated it aloud: "'Where once Mount Krakatoa stood the sea now plays.' How tragic. Do they number the fatalities?"

"Unknown," answered Pierce. Then he gripped the paper tight enough to cause a crease. "How ridiculous."

I'd never considered a tragic volcanic eruption ridiculous, per se, and so I fished for an explanation. "The volcano?"

"Court circular right beside the story of Krakatoa. Who cares if the Queen went driving yesterday?"

Not a monarchist then.

I read the circular and felt I could reliably report that Princess Beatrice and the Dowager Marchioness of Ely cared, as they were present for the morning and afternoon drives, respectively. However, I held my silence. It did not seem the moment to indulge in what the feelings of the Dowager Marchioness of Ely may or may not be.

Pierce then remarked that after every major eruption of the last century, there have been eerily strong sunsets around the world. "I imagine we can expect the same now, for months. More likely years."

"Years?" I challenged.

"It can take years for the debris to settle."

"Will it come to London?"

"We'll certainly find out."

He had set the paper aside, and we sat unspeaking—both imagining the volcano, I presume—when the top page caught a breeze and flew across the street. Pierce stood and half limped, half jogged across the street to fetch it. When he had snagged the errant news—one hopes Princess Beatrice did not find herself dizzy from the journey—he turned, and, instead of coming right back, he paused and looked at me sitting on the steps of Lapis Lazuli.

"Don't move."

"Don't move?" An order which immediately caused me to sneeze.

"Move, but don't leave your place. I'll be right back." He walked over to Lapis Lazuli Minor, went inside, and after a few minutes came out with one of his large cameras flung over one shoulder, the other hand carrying some sort of equipment. Without a word, he crossed the street and began to set up the picture. I sat watching him, amused.

In the time it took for Pierce to ready himself to capture the scene, Tybalt had slipped through the open door of Lapis Lazuli Minor, leapt down the steps, moved as only a cat can across the sidewalk, and then was up the stairs of Lapis Lazuli House to sit beside me.

Just then, Pierce, who had disappeared beneath the black fabric of the camera, lifted the flash and said, "If I catch you making a dour face, Emma…"

Which thing made me smile. Then he said, "Hold it!" And took the photograph.

Tybalt was not impressed and more than a little startled when the flash went off, and so I gathered him up in my arms and nuzzled the side of his face. He could not decide between purr and aggrieved complaint. In the time I'd held Tybalt captive, Pierce had loaded the powder in his flash, and with no warning he took a second photograph—in the exact moment a swallow dove in front of me and Tybalt leapt for it!

Following the ill-fated bird, Tybalt disappeared into the small garden on the side of the house.

"Bloody brilliant," I heard Pierce say from across the street.

"You'll have nothing but a blur!"

He shrugged. It was much like his other movements, as if he'd purchased it from humanity and was its sole possessor. Ah, Niall Pierce, owning pieces of life without realising he's even done it.

"I trust serendipity," he said.

"Oh, I wouldn't," I answered. "Serendipity has seen me into more scrapes than I care to tell."

He smiled, then picked up his camera and walked towards me, favouring his bad leg.

Does it hurt? I wanted to ask.

I didn't.

Pierce put away his camera, returned, sat back down, and we both began reading through the rest of his newspaper, talking lightly of nothing as the afternoon walked by.

August 31st

No wonder I'm exhausted.

It is more than an inch thick. The last two months of my journal.

I'm sitting up at Primrose Hill seeking solitude and the cool air London has welcomed—finally!

Tonight is Lady Trewartha's dinner.

Having the traditional Aunt Eugenia-mandated Season end at the Duchess of Bedford's ball, I'm trying to decide—

Oh dear. Look who it is.

One would think I'm cursed.

Unfair, as I've not disturbed a single Egyptian tomb…that I know of.

Later

He sat down uninvited. A thing I reminded him of when he asked, with an air of retribution, "Is that your *personal* journal, Miss Lion?"

"It may be, Islington."

"I should demand you hand it over."

"Certainly not."

"And what is that section you are holding there between your fingers with such a dogged expression?"

"It may or may not be the last two very trying months of my life."

He raised a ducal eyebrow. "All of that? July and August? Either your summers are far more extraordinary than mine, or you must think highly of your comings and goings."

"Islington?"

"Yes?"

"I have maimed lesser men."

That brought about a laugh and an unexpected slip of the formal expression he so often uses when sending a barbed comment my way. "I'm glad to know there are men out there you still deem lesser than I."

"You have your qualities."

"That sounded painful to admit."

"It wasn't. I know you're in possession of a few, most found in your unique handwriting. I still wonder how you learnt such a thing."

Nothing moved in Islington's attitude, not a hair caught by the breeze, nor the twitch of a finger, save a quick pull around his eyes. "My sister and I. We were mad for distinctive calligraphy."

"So you invented your own?"

He gave no answer.

We sat silent for a full thirty seconds before he asked, "Why trying?"

"Excuse me?"

"The last two months have been trying? Is it your cousin?"

I leaned against the back of the bench and looked down towards London. Does one confide in Islingtons? What exactly are their uses? I seem to be stuck with one of my own, so I should find out. Being a duke rules out certain possibilities, but I've a haunted photographer for life's real problems, and scoundrel Jack, were I to need anything illegal. So the question remains...what does one do with an Islington? Putting the question aside for later study, I turned to generalities.

"Yes, no," I answered in a noncommittal way. "Among other things."

We sat.

I considered the Great Islington Question.

Then he stood.

"Until this evening."

"This evening?"

"You were sent an invitation to Lady Trewartha's soirée, were you not?"

"I was."

"Then I repeat, until this evening."

And he left.

I watched him go with two thoughts twining around one another. The first, a defence against his slight of my effusive journal keeping. (Effusive? I think not. There has been much to report. I cannot help if Islington finds his Julys and Augusts unremarkable. For mine have felt worth remarking on. And were I to insert footnotes into the endeavour of recording my life—yes, I've been tempted—I would insert one now that reads: Islington, no great exemplar of brevity in his own writings—and to that I can testify.)

What else was I thinking…? Oh yes, the second thought occupying my mind. My particular specie of Islington seems to find great pleasure in treating our every conversation as if it were a fencing match. Subtle, yes, and with dignity as stiff as his collar, but a spar, nonetheless.

I always feel as if I'm holding a sword when he's left.

I shall have to remember to bring one to the dinner party.

Later

I've just returned from Lady Trewartha's.

It is nearly three o'clock in the morning.

I suppose there is no sense in penning an introduction to the affair. It will simply have to be recorded as best I can remember, then fully scrutinized in a day or two when my headache—temperance, you fool, temperance!—has fled.

I'll forget too many details, but I might as well attempt it. Otherwise, there can be no sense made of how the extraordinary night came to an end.

I hired a hansom cab to take me to Baron's Square. It's not a far walk, but it is uphill, and I was reluctant to arrive at Lady Trewartha's dinner in a less than flattering state. I still had no idea as to why I'd been invited in the first place.

When Archibald heard from Parian that I had been?

Well.

Our neighbour, Mr. Johnston, rushed over to see if he could be of assistance. Seeing that no one was being murdered, he thought he might try and appease the old man. I believe I promised Mr. Johnston that if his wife could not remove the raspberry jam, sustained when a piece of toast was lobbed in his direction, I would recompense him for a new shirt.

It took me an hour to decide what I should wear. Agnes thought the shimmering gown I'd worn for the Bedford Ball.

Emma M. Lion was tempted.

However, I was uncertain if it was the most appropriate. The invitation did not suggest dancing, only dinner and entertainment. I didn't wish to stand out before I knew what I was standing in.

I settled on the midnight blue.

Agnes helped with my unruly hair.

While not tame, it did not appear feral, so three cheers for that.

The hansom delivered me to Lady Trewartha's doorstep. Someone in livery opened the front door; someone in livery led me to a large drawing room. My strategy was simple: enjoy myself a great deal while keeping my own company. It seemed sound. It felt possible.

At that moment, I wished my friend Saffronia March was already home, for, as she is one of St. Crispian's more interesting individuals, I would assume she would have been invited.

The room was full of them. The rich. The interesting.

I am neither.

Our hostess was, to my trained eye, absent.

Well!

Steeling myself and, to my own surprise, uttering thanks to Aunt Eugenia for the social knowledge she's foisted upon me, I smiled my way through the room without speaking to anyone, looking to all the world as if I Belonged.

The far corner of the room turned refuge—fewer lights, more shadows—and I settled in to watch the other animals in this impromptu kingdom.

Then came the scent of storm on the horizon. For who should walk into the drawing room? Niall Pierce. Who apparently moves in the most unexpected heights and breadths of London's social strata. He looked striking, his limp as invisible as it could be. And those gathered in the room turned, as if catching the change in the breeze, the pressure of the air altering around them.

I smiled.

But instead of the room subjecting itself to his weather, a strange phenomenon occurred. His grey cloud presence was brought into an unexpected order, as if set in a painting of storm and shipwreck for others to admire.

And admire they did.

Our hostess appeared and made introductions. Taller than nearly every other man in the room, he nodded, gave half-smiles, polite and pleasing, as the circumstances required.

Where he learned it, I'll never know.

Eventually he lifted his eyes, sensing he was being watched by more than strangers, and found me in my corner. Like a spy.

His eyes crinkled.

I grinned.

It was nice to be found out by a friend.

A few more exchanges, and he too sought refuge in my corner.

"Well met," I said.

"Well met, indeed."

"How are you found among Lady Trewartha's menagerie?"

His fingers twitched as if he wished he were holding a drink. "I took her portrait earlier this month. A friend of a friend made the recommendation. When she found out I lived in St. Crispian's, she sent me an invitation. You?"

"I've no idea. I didn't think she even knew I existed. I'm not an Interesting, as yourself. And the closest I've ever been to *Debrett's*—where she ranks rather highly—was standing on a copy to spy on Roland when I was nine."

"Perhaps you are to be offered on the altar of St. Crispian's. The virgin sacrifice to ensure good crops and Roman ghosts."

"Ha!" And then I felt the nagging worry he may be right. "Will you enjoy your evening, do you think?" I asked.

"It will be like many others, and I'll be pleasantly bored."

"It is St. Crispian's," I warned. "However, I expect you may be right. Let us claim this corner and hold it against the Huns until dinner."

It must be repeated that he was very striking in his evening kit. I told him so.

"Thank you. May I return the compliment?"

"Certainly."

It was then I saw the ghost of noonday past.

Islington. His cool features hardly shifting as he politely shook hands. It did not take extraordinary intelligence to gather he was making his way towards me.

"Oh dear," I said aloud.

"What is it?" Pierce asked.

"Rather whom. A friend of mine."

Pierce paused. Then, "Do you anticipate all friends with such trepidation?"

"Only those who disapprove of me," I answered.

Narrowing his eyes in amusement, Pierce smiled. "That must be the majority then?"

Before I could make a righteous Old Testament sort of reply, Islington had arrived.

"Miss Lion," he said, coolly assessing.

"Hello, Islington. I didn't realise you put yourself on public display so often. Twice in one day."

Islington gave no answer, simply tried to make me uncomfortable.

I turned towards good manners to carry the day. "May I introduce Mr. Pierce? Mr. Pierce, the Duke of Islington."

They shook hands.

Then the very manly:

"Call me Islington, please."

"Certainly. I go by Pierce."

It was then that Islington performed a sort of miracle. He surprised me.

"Pierce? Niall Pierce? The photographer?"

Pierce confirmed his identity with a nod, and Islington, of all things, looked impressed.

"I have long been an admirer of your work." And he extended his hand again, as if a second handshake could convey his admiration.

Pierce shook it, answering, "That's not a comment I hear every day."

"I didn't say your work was comfortable. But yours is one of the most memorable exhibitions I've ever seen."

"Which did you attend?"

"Paris, '81. I was hoping to speak with you, but you were, ah, unavailable."

(There was his *ah*. Dreadful weapon.)

Pierce laughed. "I was at that. A kind way of saying 'indisposed.'"

Islington's answering smile was wry. "Quite."

In that moment I felt a touch of…nervousness? Joy? Panic?

I was highly entertained at their strange connection.

I was absolutely uncertain if I wanted it to happen.

Whyever not? I asked myself.

This went through my mind as Islington asked Pierce, "Are you in London for long?"

To which Pierce answered, "I've just set up a studio. Portraiture."

"War photographer no more?"

"I still intend to follow the campaigns, spend a few months of the year here and there, but I thought I would turn my focus towards something more pedestrian. And whatever roots I can scrape together."

"I can imagine. Where are you staying?"

"Here in St. Crispian's, actually. I am letting Lapis Lazuli Minor from Miss Lion. She is my landlord. Landlady, I mean."

Landlady.

That is what he called me.

How very mature it made me sound; forty, round, and red-faced.

He saw me raise my eyebrow and had the grace to smile as he raised one in return.

Meanwhile, Islington was studying me as if I were chief suspect in a murder.

Having absorbed the information of my role in Pierce's life, he said a touch dryly, "All roads lead to Rome."

Honestly.

"I did warn you that fate has its way with me, Islington."

"Yet I wonder if your mischief rules even fate."

"Oh no. It is too wild a thing for me. I'm developing a distrust of the entire enterprise," I answered. "But believe what you must."

It was then Lady Trewartha took control of the room in an unorthodox fashion. Instead of a dinner gong, she clapped her hands together. "Welcome, friends. We've a long evening ahead of us—I saw that, General Braithwaite—and I promise enjoyment for all. Now, without ceremony, follow me to the conservatory."

The duke, I expected, would be one of the first to leave the room, but he stood with Pierce and myself while the guests funnelled out. I bit my tongue, though heaven and hell both know I wished to tease him about mingling with the unwashed masses.

"Pierce, why are we going to the conservatory?" I whispered.

"I suspect that is where we will find the altar upon which you will be sacrificed," he replied.

Islington overheard, for he glanced at Pierce. "Is Miss Lion being sacrificed on our behalf?"

"For queen and country," drawled Pierce.

"The gods might wish for a more contrite soul," Islington added.

"Then you should climb atop yourself, Islington. I'm certain the gods would be most willing to take you."

This produced an unexpected smile.

The conservatory looked enchanting in the summer evening, bursting with palms and ferns, candles everywhere, with circular tables suggesting room for four or five guests scattered about. There were no place cards. Instead, Lady Trewartha stood in the doorway and sent us each to ~~an assigned seat~~ our doom, creating smaller, more intimate dining experiences.

Many present were longtime friends accustomed to the arrangement. One table consisted of four laughing women, for example, whose four smiling husbands had been seated on the far side of the conservatory. An apparent relief to both parties.

As I was flanked by Islington and Pierce, who had returned to speaking of Paris in '81, Lady Trewartha greeted us, gave each of us a discerning look and proclaimed:

"Islington, do you know Mr. Pierce?"

"We've only just met, although I've long been an admirer of his work."

"Is that so? I've just discovered our new resident and must say I'm enchanted with the portraits he took of me. You must see them before you go. Why don't the two of you settle at that table there, with Mrs. Rushton and her daughter. They are very deep in the London art scene, yet I promise are not dim-witted. A rare exception, I know. I expect you both to enjoy their company and considerable charm. Off you go."

And she waved them away.

Towards the Mrs. and Miss Rushton.

Of whom I know nothing about save the following:

Mrs. Rushton is a handsome woman.

Miss Rushton is a beautiful young woman.

They both appeared to be a frustrating combination of intelligence and beauty.

Pierce had the grace to glance back to where I stood, quite abandoned.

I felt, well, indignant!

Offended somehow, deprived of my company.

And thought, with a Lady Eugenia Spencer disapproval of the chin, that it is a thankless world in which we live.

Lady Trewartha turned to me. Her dark curls were marbled with silver, high cheekbones and violet eyes giving her the feeling of endless vitality. She was a handsome woman. "Miss Lion, you must think me terribly rude, as Islington is superb company and your Mr. Pierce devilishly handsome (*my* Mr. Pierce?); however, I have something in mind which I think will give you tremendous fun. Allow me to send you to that table over there."

She pointed to the far corner, a larger table set for ten or so, flanked by palms and candelabra. The only thing was, there was no one sitting *at* the table. It was a sparkling array of silver and crystal and nothing.

"As highly as I think of my own company, Lady Trewartha—" I began.

My hostess actually laughed. "Ah, Miss Lion, you do your parents credit. No, I was about to invite you to refresh yourself in the powder room. Claim a few moments for yourself, and if my timing is right, you will return to worthwhile companions. I've given you my *favourite* spot. Off with you."

As doubtful as Thomas, I did as I was bade.

I went to the powder room, freshened up as much as I was able, realised my wild hair had escaped a few pins (making me look rather like an 1830s heroine), gave up trying to rearrange it, picked up a magazine, read an article about a woman who embezzled forty thousand pounds from her charitable society (forty thousand pounds!), and returned to the conservatory.

Admittedly, I was nervous the table would still be conspicuously empty and the Ladies Rushton—with their exalted taste in art—would look at me through their opera glasses (why they should have them at a formal dinner, I don't know, but my imagination thought them a justified addition) and laugh as I sat alone.

My demise felt certain.

However.

As I returned to the conservatory, I saw that my table was now fully populated.

With men.

Young men.

A great number of them.

A small effort of the recollective variety placed their faces. The Last Row at Select Church Services, also known as the Traitors Road Set. Young Hawkes's friends from his Cambridge days.

The butler appeared at my elbow and said, "Miss Lion, might I see you to your seat?"

"Uh, certainly."

He did, and the ruckus—which I later learned was Cambridge for "general conversation"—continued around me as the butler pulled out my chair, saw me seated, and then abandoned me in this den of exuberant males. Some were sitting, some were standing, all were arguing about something. It took a moment for them to realise I was at the table at all.

"Oh, hello!"

"By Jove! A female."

"Lovely. How do you do?"

"Anyone know her name?"

"You can just ask her. She's sitting right there."

"Can't. I lost a bet to Foxy, and now I can't speak to any woman until the seventh of next month."

Laughter. And then the fellow at my right put out his hand and said, "Striker, for all intents and purposes. And you are?"

"Undecided if I'll release that information," I answered.

"Bravo!" called a young man who was standing, with one foot on his chair, an unlit cigarette dangling from his mouth.

"A game then?" said Striker. "We like games. We shall have to figure out who you are on our own. In the meantime, let me introduce my friends. To your left is Capper. Then we have Quality Jones, Sargent, The Boy, Mastiff, Charlie Cross, Odysseus, Night Watchman, and me, Striker. Collectively, we are the Ten Pound Note, rather more formally known as The Reprobates Ten."

By the time he had finished said introduction, I had abandoned any other expression than absolute delight. It was impossible to not be charmed. "The Reprobates Ten?" I answered. "But there are only nine of you."

"Oh no, we've one more."

"Who might that be?" I asked.

"Who?" Night Watchman said, "Why only the finest—"

"The freshest—"

"The upstanding—"

"The one and only—"

And then, all in unison, "The Mighty Nigel Hawkes!"

And the great cheer that went up brought about two things: First, all the other guests glanced around their respective plants towards our table, then, seeing who it was, turned back to their more polite conversations. Second, as if we were all participating in an unruly séance, Young Hawkes stepped into the conservatory. Which caused another cheer from our corner.

Young Hawkes looked slightly pained at the invariable glances in his direction, but there was a glint in his eye as he was greeted by Lady Trewartha and sent our way. He claimed the empty seat between Mastiff and Charlie Cross and gave me a quick nod from across the table.

"No revealing her name, Mighty Nigel Hawkes," Striker ordered. "We're going to guess."

Hawkes made no acknowledgement as he settled back into his chair.

"My question is," said Sargent, "who is she, to be sent to The Reprobates' Table?"

"Is that what it is officially called?" I asked. "The Reprobates' Table?"

"Yes."

"Certainly."

"What else should it be called?"

"By you all or our hostess?" I further enquired.

"Both," Striker said.

Hawkes cleared his throat and started fiddling with the edge of his napkin. "It is, indeed, known as The Reprobates' Table."

Well.

A public labelling of my person. Cousin Archibald's dream come true.

"So why is our mystery woman sent here to be among us?" The Boy asked Hawkes.

Hawkes looked like an explanation was inevitable. "Because her exploits make you gentlemen look like schoolboys."

A cry of general disbelief sounded, and the scepticism of my own expression drew a quiet smile from Hawkes. He lifted his hand in a blameless manner. "Your cousin confesses a great deal when I visit. I heard about the *Jane Eyre* escapade two weeks past."

"He couldn't possibly know anything about that!" I told him.

Hawkes's eyes carried a challenge. "Perhaps. Perhaps not. The picture he painted was rather fantastical. The words that come to mind are unchaperoned, questionable company, breaking and entering, drugging of the innocent, theft, and, er, gloating—if his account is to be believed."

I sat with my mouth agape.

How could Cousin Archibald have *possibly* known any of that?

How?

There was a mumble of approval round the table, and the young man I believe to be Charlie Cross said, "Gentlemen, we are in the presence of greatness."

And they held a moment of silence for me, heads bowed, hands extended in admiration. It felt very Egyptian Goddess, surrounded by her acolytes.

Hawkes, of course, was the notable exception. He sat in his seat looking very holy, leaving all pagan worship to his associates.

It was enough of a spectacle that the entire conservatory took note.

Niall Pierce, from his far corner of the earth, caught my eye and raised an eyebrow at the scene.

I shrugged.

He smiled.

Islington was either mildly amused or mildly disapproving. One cannot say for sure.

"Enough, you reprobates," I ordered. "Do you mean to ruin my reputation entirely?"

As it happens, they didn't.

Order was restored.

Dinner was then served.

Seven courses.

The conversation was an absurd melee of jests and opinions.

Their attempts to guess my identity soon deteriorated into throwing out various names to see what stuck.

"Mable!"

"Catherine!"

"Violet!"

"Not Violet, you fool. She looks more like a Cassandra."

"Eloise!"

"Elizabeth?"

"Agatha!"

"Agatha?" I challenged.

Hawkes, of course, sat above it all, focused on the meal before him, his dishevelled hair looking wonderful for wear in the candlelight.

Not long after, The Reprobates Ten gave up, decided to call me Mary, Queen of Scots, and began to comment on the people present. They went table by table, making humorous—and, on occasion, wholly inappropriate—remarks.

When The Reprobates arrived at Islington and Pierce's table, they said nothing about the women, instead praising the duke.

"I've no idea who that other chap may be," began The Boy, "but Islington there is the paragon of the single man. Wealthy. Attractive. A whip at cards. Always picks the winning horse. Invited to everything. Liked by everyone. But strangely distant from it all."

"He's the man we would all be if we weren't fantastically happy being ourselves," grinned Striker.

"I'd be him in a second," muttered Mastiff.

The Boy laughed as he passed his unlit cigarette from one hand to the other, and the others took it in stride, this making a good deal of fun of themselves.

I was trying desperately not to laugh, but when I looked to Hawkes for commiseration, he was leaning back with his eyes closed, arms crossed, seemingly oblivious to it all.

It was during the dessert course that I noticed Islington making his way towards us.

Striker gave a whistle, and the attention of every Reprobate followed the signal. The whispers began.

"Demigod!"

"The legend."

"Good for the Gold."

"By Jove. He's coming over!"

Hawkes opened his eyes, silently acknowledged the absurd reverence which had descended, offered me a single nod as if to say this was a common occurrence, and closed his eyes again.

Islington addressed me.

"I was commissioned by our hostess to enquire after your musical talents, Miss Lion." Then with a mean edge, "Do you have any?"

At the mention of my name, a general groan went up from the table. Dejection on every face.

Islington cast his eyes over The Reprobates with a degree of derision.

"You've ruined their fun, Islington," I said. "They've spent the better part of two hours trying to guess my name."

"Fools and their entertainments are soon parted," Islington replied, with what I thought was a rather cold tone. Young Hawkes mouthed a silent, *Amen*.

"But we've yet to guess her Christian name!" Quality Jones interjected.

A cheer went up.

Then Islington, knowing full well what he was doing, said, "Well, Emma?"

The Reprobates let out a second round of groans.

"You really are a killjoy, Islington," I said.

His hazel-eyed stare indicated he couldn't have cared any less.

"Do not delay my errand, Miss Lion," Islington pressed. "You? Musical ability? Do the twain meet?"

"Only in appreciation, I'm afraid."

"Very well, then. I shall carry your report to our hostess," Islington replied. He looked severely around the table. "A word of warning. If any of these jokers try to get you to stake anything of value on whist, don't waste your time. They play like fools and set their stakes in the same manner. Hawkes excluded, obviously."

After he walked away from the table, The Reprobates all burst into laughter.

"Finest fellow in St. Crispian's, Hawkes the Fox excepted."

"Capital sort of man."

"A real shine."

"And he seems to know our own Mary, Queen of Scots well enough!"

"Emma," Capper—or was it Sargent?—corrected. "Emma Lion."

"*Miss*," Night Watchman emphasized.

"She is not *Miss* to any of you," said Hawkes, eyes still closed.

Striker took the lead. "Miss Lion is known to Islington, funny, lovely, and, according to the good word of Mighty Nigel Hawkes, has her own history of derring-do. I think we've found ourselves a Maid Marian!"

A cheer arose.

Hawkes opened his eyes. He caught Striker's eye and shook his head.

"No? How about a Scheherazade?"

Again Hawkes signalled no.

"Why not Maid Marian?" I asked, but no one heard me.

"A Bloody Mary?"

This time Hawkes drew his eyebrows together in disapproval.

"If she's not a Bloody Mary, surely she's an Eleanor of Aquitaine!" stated Quality Jones.

Hawkes did not dissent.

"Aquitaine?" I asked, very confused. But Charlie Cross spoke over me.

"Gentlemen. We've found a lucky penny. A regular E of A, Miss Emma Lion. All for it, say Aye."

There were nine Ayes.

Hawkes didn't vote.

"Come on, Hawkes."

"I abstain on the grounds I am Miss Lion's spiritual leader."

"Ah yes."

"A bit sticky that."

"You mean because she's—that you—and if there was?"

"Precisely," said Young Hawkes.

"It's unanimous then!"

"Have I not a vote?" I objected. "I'm not going to be an E of A for anyone without knowing the consequences."

"Sorry. Members only and that sort of thing."

In that very moment, all guests were invited by Lady Trewartha into the music room.

As I stood, The Reprobates Ten—a muddle of shouts and amusements—rose around me, and I was swept through the conservatory in their midst.

Hawkes disappeared. And did not, I must make note, reappear the entire evening.

At the door, I was picked off.

I don't quite know how they did it, but Pierce and Islington were standing near the threshold, hands in their pockets, talking about something, and one of them simply reached out and pulled me out of the centre of "the heathens with whom I'd eaten dinner"—a direct quote from Islington.

"Hello, Emma," Pierce said as I found myself at his side. "You are obviously welcome to follow your exuberant companions, but Islington and I would also request your company. If you would care to join us for the music?"

I looked towards the music room with not a small amount of relief. "They are delightful in small doses. Like a litter of puppies, one would suspect."

"Don't romanticize them," Islington muttered.

We found a sofa near the back. There was enough seating for all the ladies and most of the men, and so I somehow managed to find myself seated in the middle, Pierce and Islington on either side.

It was a strange evening, a musical revue of sorts. Some excellent performers, including one professional pianist—the high point of the night—and a rambunctious number performed by The Reprobates—dedicated to yours truly.

"Why did they call you Eleanor of Aquitaine?" Pierce whispered.

"Because I'm their Lucky Penny," I said with a matter-of-fact tone.

The music wore on, or so I believe, for I fell into a doze only to be woken by Pierce, whose shoulder I had borrowed.

But was the evening over? No. For there were games and drinks and general conversation. A lot of "Heavens, have we met?" and "Ah look, I see Lady so-and-so."

General Braithwaite recognised me and monopolized a fair amount of my time. Islington was invited to see Lady Trewartha's portrait, a thing I'd hoped not to miss. Alas. The general had decided to disclose the entire history of his third decade. The Mrs. and Miss Rushton, I observed, had found their way to Pierce's side once more.

As a rule, dislike should be founded on more than a person simply speaking with one's friend.

As a rule.

Perhaps not an inflexible one.

Finally, the evening came to an end. It was not long before I—yawning—found myself once again in the company of Islington and Pierce (who were now discussing photography and sport) and taking leave of Lady Trewartha.

Out the front door, down the wide white steps, bidding farewell to the other guests who wandered back to their homes in Baron's Square, or down towards Sterling Street and into the rest of St. Crispian's.

Islington and Pierce were speaking of something as The Reprobates gathered round me and kissed my hands.

"A goodnight, Lucky Penny."

"Jolly night, Miss Lion."

"Tell Islington he is the Royal Mile."

"Farewell, A of E."

"Goodnight!" I called after them. (I surmise they went not home but to some club, where they gambled away a tremendous sum.)

My head was fuzzy and my feet tired—despite not having danced. And so, while the conversation turned from sport to Vienna, of all places, I wandered across the street to the fountain of my weeping Medusa and arrogant Perseus. Wholly unacceptable on any other occasion, I took off my shoes and stockings and sat on the edge of the fountain, my feet in the water.

The men, in a distracted manner, followed me, standing not ten feet away from where I sat.

And there we stayed, puddled by the fountain, I listening to the back and forth fall of the male voices, my fingers weaving through the water. At some point, my feet sufficiently wet, I turned and sat facing them.

"That was years ago," Pierce was saying. "I was in Damascus with Jonathan Revel, one of my American friends."

"It was Jonathan who introduced me to your work," came Islington's reply.

I pulled my attention away from the study of my abandoned shoes by moonlight and gave more of it to the conversation before me.

"You know Jonathan?" Pierce asked, clearly very pleased.

"I do."

"Do you know Maggie also?"

It could have been the shadows, but Islington's smile stiffened. "I do."

Pierce grinned. "I've just had a letter from Maggie telling me how well the new colts are doing."

"Is she well?"

"Of course. If you know Maggie… She's got one hell of an eye for good horses. Wins the Day is a tremendous sire for their stables."

"I'll agree with that," Islington replied.

It was then that a fan of golden light opened across the dark street, and Lady Trewartha's butler and a footman came out carrying, of all things, a platter of cheeses, bread, pastries, fruits, and a carafe of freshly-brewed coffee, three cups on the ready. They silently served as we uttered a thank you, then they left the platter on a folding table near the fountain, and returned to the house.

One would think the three of us had not enjoyed a seven-course meal only hours before. And the strange ease between us turned towards cooling our coffee and eating whatever caught our fancy.

"Do you know Maggie very well?" Islington asked at length, his sharper demeanour back in play.

"Jonathan introduced us after they were married. What, three years ago? I spent a few months with them last winter in California. Then we travelled to Maryland to tour the racing stables."

"*Ah.*"

"*Ah,*" I repeated aloud, to humour myself.

Islington glanced at me over his coffee.

"How do you know Maggie?" Pierce asked.

While sipping my coffee and eating a piece of cheese, I watched Islington calculate behind that usually unreadable face of his. Then, "Margaret is my youngest sister."

Pierce almost dropped his coffee.

And I, never having met this Maggie in my life, raised both of my eyebrows.

His sister!

What was a duke's sister doing married to an American and raising racehorses in Maryland?

I'm assuming from Pierce's expression that he wanted to know the same thing.

"You're kidding me," he laughed.

Islington said nothing.

"I'd have never thought."

"No, you wouldn't. The story is that she's abroad and, having finished with art school, is now touring Europe with a suitable elderly companion."

Pierce gave a single-syllabled guffaw. "Maggie? Following a spinster around Europe? She'd rather eat a horse saddle. She's mad for Jonathan."

"So she told me," replied the duke, "when she wrote to me from America after eloping."

Now Pierce really laughed, a thing I think was helped by the many drinks of the evening.

"Why the story that she's abroad?" I asked.

Islington set his coffee cup and napkin on the pillaged tray. "My older sister does not wish to weather the scandal. Maggie is only nineteen. In six months, she will meet an American named Jonathan Revel and, with my permission, become engaged. The decision will be had to marry in America, as his mother is ailing and would not be up for the journey. I myself will have too much work managing my estates to go, but I'll send an exquisite silver tea service with my blessing."

"Heavens," I said. "Very elaborate."

"Very proper, which my elder sister desires very much."

Silence descended. Pierce finished his coffee.

It was Islington who first glanced at his pocket watch, but Pierce was the one who ended the evening.

"It's late," he said, running a hand through his hair. "We should go. Emma?"

Islington nodded in agreement and then looked curiously from me to Pierce.

Or so I believe.

It was almost two in the morning.

And one can only interpret so many expressions in one evening.

It was on good terms—a handshake for Pierce, a pause and then a handshake for me—that we parted, Islington walking towards his house, Pierce and I to Sterling Street and down the Diagonal.

"I cannot believe Maggie is his sister," Pierce said in amusement when we were nearly home.

"Is she so unlike him?" I asked.

"I've no idea, as I've only met the man tonight, but she's a firebrand. A woman who knows her own mind. She can argue any man to the ground. I've seen her shoot a hole through an ace of hearts while riding the back of a horse."

"Goodness!" I couldn't help myself. Frankly, she sounded too mythical to be real. "How very Outlaw of the West she sounds."

"I suppose she found the place where she belongs."

We came to a stop before Lapis Lazuli.

"I suppose we all wish for that," I said.

"Hmm?" he asked, his thoughts elsewhere.

"To find where we belong. We all wish for that," I answered.

"And you? Is that what you wish for?"

I think I was afraid to really consider the question because my whole life I've believed it to be here. And so I said quickly, "But I've found it, Pierce. I belong here, at Lapis Lazuli House. It is my birthright."

"I suppose you are lucky to have found it so soon."

"I suppose I am," I confirmed.

But before I could ask if he'd found a place he belonged, Pierce ran a tired hand across his eyes.

"Is your door unlocked?" he asked.

"I believe so, but I've also a key."

Walking up the steps, I tried the doorknob. It gave way, and I opened the door.

"Goodnight, Emma," he said.

"Goodnight."

And without a second glance, he disappeared inside Lapis Lazuli Minor.

I've not heard him on the other side of the wall, so I half suppose he stopped by his studio and fell asleep.

It is now nearly three o'clock in the morning, and I'm certain to pay for my transgressions come morning.

An unexpected ending to a strange August.

Memorable.

They seemed ready friends, did they not?

Oh dear. Speaking of friends, Tybalt has just entered my side of the garret, wide-eyed, ready for a night of catching mice. I'll open the door to the west garret and let him loose to see what he can find.

As for myself, I've no desire to hunt anything other than the sweetest of dreams.

May I find them 'til morning.

THE PERSONAL LIBRARY *of* EMMA M. LION
As It Currently Stands

The Complete Works of Shakespeare by *William Shakespeare*
Illustrated by Declan Lion

The Holy Bible

Jane Eyre by *Charlotte Brontë*
Gifted by the Jane Eyre Society of Fortitude, A Preparatory School for Girls

Shakespeare's Comedies, In Full
Gifted by Roland Sutherland

Jane Eyre by *Charlotte Brontë*
Gifted by Roland Sutherland

Latin Phrases for the Unrepentant by *Barclay Stafford*
Won at The Dalliance Bookshop

Self-Reliance by *Ralph Waldo Emerson*
Gifted by Niall Pierce

Essays by *Ralph Waldo Emerson*
Gifted by Niall Pierce

Meaning of Flowers
Found in the breakfast room

Dear Reader,

As appalling as it is to read another's journal, I would like to thank all those who made it possible for you to begin reading mine.

Thank you to the family and friends of Beth Brower. She has them in abundance. They are always encouraging and believe in her. Which is the nicest of things. She specifically is grateful for the time given by Caitlin, Jenesse, Kimberly, her Mother, her Father, Rose, Alena, and Lori; your contributions are appreciated.

Thank you, Angie, who listened to the madcap plan over a cup of cocoa.

As for Rob. He tries.

Thank you, Tyson Cantrell, for allowing your lovely design to grace the cover of my journals.

Thank you, Jennifer Lerud. For your brilliant copy editing, your generosity, and your goodness. I sleep better knowing Beth has you on her side.

Thank you, Allysha Unguren, for your talents and wisdom. For sussing things out. And for weighing curious, singular, and peculiar.

Thank You, Ben Unguren, for all the magician's tricks. And for cleaning my typewriter. And for putting purple ink on the spools. You are a rare combination of the analogue and digital in this degenerate age.

Thank you, Kip. For making the good possible. And for being the best. Beth is a fool if she ever takes you for granted.

A note concerning the presumptuous Beth Brower, who thought it a good idea to put my journals into the world. She lives with the aforementioned Kip, her chemist husband, and their cat, Spy Cat Grey.

Beth enjoys citrus scents, books, handwoven rugs, and walking in any weather. She listens to songs on repeat. She feels rather fiercely about the ones she loves and needs windows for light and walls for art.

Beth Brower has written the following books:

The Queen's Gambit
The Ruby Prince
The Wanderer's Mark

The Q

The Beast of Ten

The Unselected Journals of Emma M. Lion

You can find more information on her website and Instagram.

www.bethbrower.com
@bethbrower

The Unselected Journals of Emma M. Lion: Vol. 4 is now available.

Sincerely,
Emma